A Namesake for Nathan

OTHER BOOKS BY F. N. MONJO

Indian Summer
The Drinking Gourd
The One Bad Thing About Father
Pirates in Panama
The Jezebel Wolf
Slater's Mill
The Vicksburg Veteran
The Secret of the Sachem's Tree
Rudi and the Distelfink
Poor Richard in France
Me and Willie and Pa
King George's Head Was Made of Lead
The Sea Beggar's Son
Grand Papa and Ellen Aroon
Willie Jasper's Golden Eagle
Gettysburg: Tad Lincoln's Story
Zenas and the Shaving Mill
The House on Stink Alley
Letters to Horseface
The Porcelain Pagoda

A Namesake for Nathan

BEING AN ACCOUNT OF
CAPTAIN NATHAN HALE
BY HIS TWELVE-YEAR-OLD
SISTER, JOANNA

by F. N. Monjo
drawings by Eros Keith

Coward, McCann, & Geoghegan, Inc.
New York

ACKNOWLEDGMENTS

Columbia University was able to furnish me with a copy of George Dudley Seymour's not easily obtainable *Documentary Life of Nathan Hale*. The rest of my research was done at the New York Society Library, for which reason I want to thank Sylvia C. Hilton and the staff there for all their help in this connection.

F.N.M.

Library of Congress Cataloging in Publication Data
Monjo, F N   A namesake for Nathan.
SUMMARY: Joanna Hale recounts the events of 1776 as she and her family follow the activities of her brother Nathan in the Continental Army.
1. Hale, Nathan, 1755-1776—Juvenile fiction.
2. United States—History—Revolution, 1775-1783—Juvenile fiction. [1. Hale, Nathan, 1755-1776—Fiction. 2. United States—History—Revolution, 1775-1783—Fiction] I. Keith, Eros. II. Title.
PZ7.M75Nam   [Fic]   76-58325
Printed in T   es of America

FOR MY MOTHER AND FATHER

CONTENTS

A Namesake for Nathan

PART ONE

Home on Leave

LITTLE JOE AND I have grown to be good friends. He's my little nephew, my sister Elizabeth's boy. He's a cute baby. Smart, too.

"Aren't you, Little Joe?" I say.

"Little Joe," says Little Joe.

And we both laugh.

We been watching icicles form on the eaves. Outside, it's sleeting and snowing. Cold. The shagbark hickory in the front yard is shivering in the frost. The pale afternoon sun slants in low, low over the bare trees. Downstairs, Pa is stamping back in from the barn, where he's been feeding the cows and the oxen, bedding all the creatures down for the night.

"Grandpa?" says Little Joe.

"Yes, little boy. That's Grandpa. You hear Grandpa downstairs?"

"Grandpa!" says Little Joe, and we laugh some more.

He's the most contented little boy I've ever seen, or my name's not Joanna Hale. Sometimes, I think he looks just like Dr. Sam Rose, his daddy. Except when he smiles. Then I think he looks like *me*. Me and his mamma, my sister Elizabeth. She lets me mind Little Joe for her, now and then, just as if I was his mamma.

She don't care, and I like to do it. Little Joe and me, we've got to be good friends.

"Joanna!" says Grandmother Strong. "Joanna!"

"What is it, Grandma'am?"

"You bring baby downstairs, now. Your pa wants his evening meal. Pretty soon be dark."

Grandmother Strong is the best cook in our family. Nobody can fix baked beans the way she can. So dark and sweet, with molasses. I can smell her brown bread, too, baking in the oven.

"I thought you was going to wait for Nathan, Grandma'am," I say, calling from the top of the stairs.

"I've put plenty by, for Nathan. It's keeping, in the Dutch oven. Just bring baby down to supper."

You should see our kitchen. It's full of family and steam and good smells. And there's bacon and beans and hot loaves of brown bread.

Mother Abigail is my stepmother. She and Grandmother Strong have been making apple turnovers all afternoon, for Nathan, because he's coming home on leave today. Home on leave from the army.

"Look at that baby! He's almost *blue* with cold!" says Sister Elizabeth, and she grabs Little Joe out of my arms, and sits down beside the fire, rubbing his cheeks and mothering him.

"Blue," says Little Joe.

"What in the name of goodness have you been doing with this child, up in that cold bedroom, Joanna?" says Mother Abigail.

"Just watching icicles, Mamma," I say, and everybody laughs.

"Joanna, you are my little dreamer, and no mistake,"

says Grandmother Strong, and she leans down to give me a kiss. "Never has been a December without icicles, dear."

"They're like the living streams of Zion's waters," I say, "froze up, and still."

"They are," says Mother Abigail. "So they are, kind of like."

I like my second mother, Mother Abigail, almost as much as I think I would have liked my own ma who used to be. I can hardly remember Ma, for I was just a little more than three when she died.

"What must a man do to hev his supper?" says Pa, calling from the keeping room. "Every critter out back has his evening meal amply spread before him, and I mean to hev *mine*."

"The whole lot of us are working to serve you, Deacon Hale," calls Grandmother Strong. "Be patient but a moment more, and you're satisfied."

"I've no great store of patience," says Pa, looking stern over his mug of cider. "And I can't abide delay."

"It's patience, nevertheless, Richard, or it's raw bacon," says Mother Abigail. "Supper's on the fire. Soon's it's cooked, we'll gladly dish it up."

Very soon after, we're all at the table. We're a big family, even today, with only half of us here.

"Bountiful Lord God," says Pa, "bless this food to our use, and us to Thy service. And extend Thy mercy, Lord God Jehovah, over my boys, absent from us in the army, in this fearful war. There's six of them, soldiers, Lord. There's Samuel to watch over, and John, and Joe. There's Richard and Billy. And there's Nathan, who I'd hoped would be supping with us

(15)

tonight. And with us here we got my son Enoch, the man of God, and my young son David, and my son-in-law, Dr. Sam Rose, to remember. He's a soldier, too. And as for the rest of us, here to home, there's my infinitely good mother-in-law, Elizabeth Strong, the best of Thy servants. And my dear wife, Abigail. And my daughters, Elizabeth and little Joanna. And my devoted daughter-in-law, Sally. And my beautiful bereft and widowed stepdaughter, Alicia. And my baby grandson, Little Joe Rose. And myself, Thy servant, Deacon Richard Hale. There's every one of us, Lord God Jehovah, craves Thy concern, Thy merciful guidance, and Thy everlasting protection, Amen."

Then Pa sits down, and Mother Abigail begins serving the food.

I miss all the tender green things we have in summertime. But it's December, now, and we won't have anything fresh, again—except milk and butter—until spring.

"Everyone eat hearty," says Grandmother Strong. "I set aside a-plenty for Nathan."

"I hope Nathan may get here soon," says Alicia, pulling her little black widow's cap over her bright hair.

"So do I," says Mother Abigail. "I hate to think of him traveling all that way on foot, in this sleet and snow."

"It's still a few minutes to full dark," says Pa. "David, you light a lantern and leave it out front, on the shagbark hickory."

"Yes, sir," says David, and off he goes for the lantern.

(16)

"I vow, Alicia, it will be nearly a year, now, since Elijah died," says Mother Abigail.

"My poor husband," says Alice. "I still wear mourning, as you see, Sister Sally. 'Twas just a year ago this day he died."

"December twenty-six," says Grandmother Strong. "A year ago today. But we must look on the bright side, too. Come this Sad'day, it's two years, December thirtieth, since Elizabeth and Dr. Sam Rose was married."

"Come Saturday," says Sister Rose, with a smile over to Dr. Sam.

"Elijah died of the lung fever," says Alice, "and the same lung fever killed my little son, Elijah, too, not a month ago."

"My little daughter," says Mother Abigail, with a kiss for Alice's cheek. "Widowed at eighteen. Widowed and bereft of her baby son. It don't seem like the Lord could have *meant* it to happen that way."

"The Lord Jehovah giveth. And the Lord Jehovah taketh away," says Pa, frowning down. "Blessed be the name of the Lord God Jehovah."

"Amen. Blessed be His name," says Enoch, real ministerlike. "We are here but a moment, in the sight of the Lord, Mother Abigail. Then we are cut down, like grass."

Pa and Enoch scare me some, when they talk that way about the Lord God Jehovah. But Enoch is studying to be a minister, at Yale, so I calculate he ought to know Jehovah's ways. And Pa's a deacon in Reverend Huntington's Congregational Church here in Coventry, Connecticut, so he must know, too. But it don't seem like Pa and Enoch miss the dead half as much as we womenfolk do. Lord knows I love my Mother Abigail, and she's been kind as a mother can be to all us ten Hale children. But I never *will* stop missing my own ma. Even though I can hardly remember her now. She's been dead near eight years, come April twenty-first. And I can't forget my little brother Jonathan, and my baby sister, Susannah, neither. All dead. I never will stop missing the three of them, no matter what Pa and Enoch say about the Lord God Jehovah, and how he cuts us down, like grass. Their graves look shady and peaceful, though, in summer, all covered over with green.

"It's my opinion," says Dr. Sam Rose, "Nathan must have decided to put up somewhere on the road, tonight, 'count of all this snow."

"I do hope he's all right," says Grandmother Strong.

"All right," says Little Joe, from his high chair, slapping a spoonful of his cornmeal mush on his chin.

Sister Rose turns and smiles at her baby.

"Dr. Sam, that boy of yours is a rascal. He's full of the mischief," says Pa.

"Yes, sir, he is that," says Dr. Sam, and Elizabeth kind of blushes, and laughs, too.

"Mischief!" says Little Joe, when Elizabeth wipes his mouth on his bib, and Grandmother Strong laughs the loudest of us all.

"Nathan is bound to be all right, Mother," says Pa, helping Grandmother Strong to another slice or two of bacon. "Never was a weakling, from the time he was a boy."

"Said he hoped to make it here from Cambridge in four days," says David, "and this is the fourth day."

"Ayeh," says Pa, "and here he is now, or I miss my guess."

There is a clumping of heavy boots on the front porch, stamping off the snow. Grandmother Strong pushes back from the trestle table, and we all get up and start for the door.

"Well, I declare!" says Pa. "It's Lieutenant Hale, of the Seventh Connecticut, come to pay us a visit!"

"Beg your pardon, sir," says Nathan, in his big hearty voice. He bangs the door behind him, and he's grinning. "I have the honor to announce that *Captain* Nathan Hale presents his compliments to all and sundry."

And Nathan starts unbuttoning his heavy coat, while Mother Abigail and Grandmother Strong and Elizabeth and Sarah and me all begin fussing around him. All of us are a-bustling, except Alice Ripley, who looks kind of pale and quiet, in her widow's black.

"So they made you captain," says Dr. Sam Rose. "Time they showed some sense."

"General Washington's to be congratulated on his choice," says Pa, real solemn, and Nathan and Enoch and David and Dr. Sam laugh, and all of us women kind of blush and smile.

"We was hoping you'd git here this evening, before dark, Nathan, dear," says Grandmother Strong.

"And here I am, honored grandma'am, as good as my word," says Nathan. First he kisses her hand, then he gives her a big hug, and finally he bends over and kisses her cheek.

"Grandma'am made her apple turnovers," says Sally, "for the returning hero."

(19)

"And baked beans and bacon and brown bread," says Mother Abigail.

"And here's a posset of good hot cider," says Pa, pouring a mug for Nathan.

"God be thanked you're home safe, brother," says Enoch.

"I believe you're limping, Nathan," says David.

"Ayeh," says Nathan, kind of slow. "I come down most of the way with Sergeant Sage, walking through snow, ankle deep. My right heel went lame."

"Let me remove your right boot, Captain Hale," says Alice, "and put that injured foot in some hot water."

"My dear Mrs. Ripley," says Nathan, "I would think it a great kindness, and that's a fact."

Nathan kind of eases himself into his seat at the table, and Alice goes hurrying into the kitchen to heat water. She calls for David to drag a tub over to the table. In no time, they have Nathan's foot soaking in warm water, and there's a steaming plate of food in front of him, and all of us are back at the table with him, having supper together, as happy as clams at high tide.

"There's only one thing requisite to make this an ambrosial feast for the gods," says Nathan, as he starts in on his baked beans.

"I know, Nathan. I remember," I say, and I run over to the cupboard, to the big stone crock. I come running back with two or three big lumps of maple sugar in a brown bowl.

"Thank you, sister Joanna," says Nathan. "A bit of sweetness helps take away the cold."

"By the great horn spoon!" says Grandmother

Strong. "The beans are sweet as sweet can be, with all the molasses I poured in, Captain Hale."

"Nothing like a bit of *maple* sweetening, honored madam," says Nathan, with a grin, as he crumbles a big lump of maple sugar over his baked beans.

"I see soldiering and General Washington ain't spoiled your appetite, nor your sweet tooth, none," says Pa, kind of grumpy. But I know he ain't really displeased at all.

It sure is good to see Nathan enjoy his meal, and to have him back with us, laughing and joking.

"You been subjecting General Howe to some unpleasantness, up there to Boston?" says Enoch. Howe's the new British general who took over from General Gage last October. And Gage is the one we started shooting at last April, at Lexington and Concord and Bunker Hill.

"General Washington has General Howe as close surrounded as the shell fits 'round an egg," says Nathan. "And we been bringing cannon, from New York, all the way across the state of Massachusetts, by ox teams. Dragging those big guns through the snow, on sleds, the whole way from Fort Ticonderoga, where Ethan Allen and his Green Mountain Boys took 'em away from the British. Soon's we have them cast-iron arguments for independence set up real solid, on Dorchester Heights, pointing down on Boston, then you'll see old General Howe start moving out in a hurry."

"You look mighty fit and healthy, Nathan," says Pa.

"Should be," says Nathan. "Been going ice skating. Eating just fine. And every week, we wrestle some, just to work up a good sweat. And my waiter there in camp, he's been taking good care of me—except for maple sugar," says Nathan, and he winks at me and crumbles another lump of sweetness into his plate of baked beans. "Only trouble we been having," says Nathan, "is the cold weather, and the fever in camp. That, and the worry over reenlistments. Now, you take my waiter. His enlistment's up, and nothing I could do would convince him to sign up for another six months. 'No, sir, Captain Hale,' he said. 'I be going back to my farm in Stonington,' and back he went. Which reminds me, I mean to ask Asher Wright to join up and be my waiter, if he'll be persuaded."

"Well, now . . ." says Pa.

"Asher?" says David. "He just might do it, Nathan. He's a great one for wrestling, too. I imagine he's pinned near everybody around Coventry, by now."

Asher Wright lives right over on the next farm. Sometimes the Wrights come over here and help us, haying and such, in July.

But Nathan's still talking about soldiering.

"Most of the soldiers," says he, "signed up for just six months, last May or June, right after Lexington. Now it's December, and their period of service is over. If they won't sign up for another hitch, General Washington stands to lose most of his volunteer army. And then the siege of Boston will be over, before we get a chance to pinch General Howe's tail with all them cannon from Ticonderoga."

"You must *strenuously* endeavor to get the men to reenlist, Captain Hale," says Alice Ripley, real severe, looking down into her dark widow's skirts.

"That is one of the purposes of my month's furlough,

Mrs. Ripley," says Nathan. "I'll be going on down to Norwich and New London and thereabouts, trying to get soldiers to reenlist, and trying to find some new recruits, too."

"Will you take more beans, Nathan?" says Grandmother Strong. "Or shall I serve you a nice pair of warm apple turnovers, with a bit of hot rum sauce? Your Pa don't let us speak of real English tea, no more. Not that I'd touch it, myself, since the troubles started. There's more hot cider, anyway, to warm you up."

"I'll say yes to them all, Grandma'am," says Nathan. "More beans, if you please. And some apple turnovers with rum sauce. And some more hot cider, too."

"That's a fine, great lad," says Grandmother Strong, and she and Mother Abigail bring Nathan everything he asked for.

The men keep talking politics: will we Yankees ever get our port city of Boston opened up to trade again? Will King George take his redcoats back to London, whence they never should have been dispatched in the first instance, or will he send yet more regulars to oppress his suffering colonies? Nathan says he hears there's *thousands* more soldiers coming over here to worry us. And Pa says it's past time we separated for good and all from insolent Britannia. Pa says we must fight to the death for all our ancient rights and liberties as free men. Of course, it ain't customary for us womenfolk to meddle in, when the men are arguing politics. So I go on clearing the table in silence, real seemly. Not that Grandma'am and Mother Abigail and Sister Rose and Alice Ripley won't speak up now and then. But it wouldn't be right for *me*—a girl that's not yet twelve.

All I know is that Pa's mighty strict and determined for separation and independence. We can't eat this, and we can't buy that, if it comes here—taxed—from England, and there's nobody firmer than Pa when his mind is made up. Pa won't even permit us to weave the wool of our own sheep into the blankets we need. He says every scrap of woolens has got to go for the use of General Washington's soldiers. So me and Sister Elizabeth Rose has been knitting stockings and mittens for Nathan and all the rest of the soldiers in the family—for Sam, and John, and Joe, and Dick, and Billy. Six of my brothers, and Elizabeth's husband, Dr. Sam Rose, all fighting against the king!

When I finish clearing the table, I go out to the kitchen to scour the plates and pots with soft soap and sand, and I help put up all the leftover food. All the women are talking of Nathan and what a great, fine man he's grown, over six feet tall now, since he went for a soldier.

"He may be but a lad of twenty," says Mother Abigail, "but he's ripened, and no mistake. He's got the strength and the wisdom of a man of thirty, now. And if he were *again* to ask for the hand of Alicia Ripley. . . ."

"Now, Mother!" says Alice, starting up, nearly overturning the crock of cider warming by the fire. "That's not to be thought of!"

"If he *were* to ask me, daughter," says Mother Abigail, fearful determined, "as he did once before, this time I think my answer'd be different. Three years ago, he was only a boy in school. *This* time I'd say Alicia might *have* him, if he pleased her."

And Alice is up the stairs in a rush, and the door to her chamber bangs shut with a thud we can hear downstairs.

"Still a little chit of a girl, widow woman though she may be," says Mother Abigail.

"You are *eternally* making matches, Mother," says Sally, "when you *know* there never was a girl in all God's creation could abide it! My sister Alice least of all!"

Grandmother Strong speaks up, real placid and considered. "Young folks may need some prodding, before coming to perceive their own true desires," says she. "I'm sure my dear and blameless Abby never meant a speck of harm to Alice. Did you, now, Abby?"

"I *meant* none, Mother," says Mother Abigail. "But time will tell if I *done* some, nonetheless."

"Nathan never wanted nobody *but* Alicia," says Sister Rose, real sharp. "And that was long before Elijah Ripley come whistling over the dale."

"Nathan was nothing but a Yale College boy, then. He was only eighteen, back in '73," says Grandmother Strong, "and Alicia was just sixteen. How would Nathan—schoolteacher that he was setting out to be, down to Haddam—how would he have been able to take himself a wife? Him not having enough money to keep *himself* in shirts and shoes. Hardly knowing how to find enough food for his own hungry mouth—let alone enough for two. But I know the truth when I hear it, Lizzie. 'Twas *always* Alicia, I'll stake my life on it."

So the men in there are talking of war and King George III. And the women talk of Alicia and Nathan out here in the kitchen. And the fire splutters, and the

(25)

snow hisses against the windows, and the deep December night closes in fast around us all.

Next morning I hear laughing, down in the snowy yard, before I'm full awake. I run over to the window and peer down through the icy panes. It's Nathan and Little Joe. Nathan has that baby swathed around and around in a long, woolen tippet, warm as can be, and can you guess what he's doing? Little Joe is riding piggy-back on Nathan's big manly shoulders! Laughing and hollering "Up-pi-dee! Up-pi-dee!" Squealing and giggling each time Nathan gives him a jounce.

And Nathan—nothing but a great big overgrown baby himself—Nathan has rolled eight huge, empty cider barrels out of the barn, and he's got them set up on end. He's got them standing in the snow, all eight of them, lined right up, one after the other. And he's got one of his great big hands holding on tight to Little Joe, and the other hand is free. And Nathan is hopping into one barrel, and then up and out of that one, and heaves himself into the next. Then another huge leap and he's into the next. Then up and out of that and into the next. All the way down the line, and back! And Little Joe squealing and hollering "Up-pi-dee!" each time Nathan bounds into the air.

I opened the window with a bang.

"Nathan!" I holler. "Have you taken leave of your senses? I thought you was supposed to be lame?"

"Me and Little Joe need *some* sport before breakfast, don't we, Joe?" says Nathan. And he plunges down that line of barrels again, shouting "Giddee-up, hoss! Giddee-up, hoss!" in that deep voice of his, with Little Joe screaming "Up-pi-dee!" like a wild Indian.

Nathan looks up at me, his face all ruddy, his blue eyes glinting in the bright morning sunlight, and his breath coming in thick white puffs on the frosty air.

"Come on down, old sleepyhead Joanna!" he yells. "Come on down and fix us some breakfast!"

Well, maybe somebody can say no to Nathan, but I can't. So I hurry into my clothes, and run downstairs to the kitchen, and start blowing up the fire with the bellows.

In no time I have some bacon frying in the spider, and a pot of cornmeal mush boiling over the flames. I take two buckets to the back door and holler out to Nathan and Little Joe.

"That's enough foolishness for one morning, *Captain* Hale! I need one of these filled with milk, and the other with water. If the well's froze up, there's rope, and an axe in the barn, for breaking the ice."

Nathan goes off, just as meek as can be, to milk the cow and fetch me the water. And Little Joe still perched on his shoulders, hollering "Hoss-ee! Hoss-ee!" and kicking his uncle in the ribs every step of the way.

I slice some brown bread for toast and cut some cheese. Next I put out a jug of molasses for the cornmeal mush, and another clean empty jug, for the fresh milk. Then I remember Nathan's going to want maple sugar 'stead of molasses, and I fetch some of that from the crock, and set it in a bowl, and put everything on the trestle table, drawn up in front of the fire.

Mother Abigail and Grandmother Strong and them are still asleep. It can't be more than five-thirty, and the sun's not full up over the trees, yet. But the sky is pink in the east and bright and clear, making all the snow pink and rosy, too. While I'm looking out, first one blue jay and then another fly up and perch on the ridgepole of the barn. I hear the oxen and the cows lowing and bellowing out there, so I know Nathan's feeding the stock. I hope he'll remember to scatter some corn for the geese and the hens. And there's sheep bleating for their hay, too.

Time Nathan gets back from the barn, my bacon's crisp and my mush is bubbling and plopping in the black iron pot hanging from the crane. The kitchen windows have turned pearly and wet with steam.

Nathan kicks the door to get me to open it for him, and he comes clumping in with two steaming pails of milk swinging from the yoke, and Little Joe still riding piggy-back, happy as a cricket on a summer day.

"So cold the milk's been smoking," says Nathan. "By now, I 'spect it's frozen."

I look at the buckets, and sakes! There's a little thin skim of ice on the surface of each one.

"I'll have to warm it up, some, for the baby," I say, "while you go get my water. And I'll need more wood for the fire."

"Respectfully at your service, Mistress Hale," says Nathan, with just a trace of mischief in his blue eyes.

"Mistress Hale or no," I say, kind of snappish, "baby needs his breakfast, now you went and waked him at this unearthly hour. So you can just be my scullery maid this morning, mister big important Captain Hale, of the Seventh Connecticut. We got no Sergeant Asher Wright, or whoever, to be waiter for *you*, here to home on the farm!"

"You talk all that vinegar, Mistress Hale," says Nathan, "and you'll wind up with the tongue in your head all pickled!"

I can't help but laugh when Nathan teases. And off he goes to the well, for the water. I set Little Joe in his high chair, and draw him up near the fire. And I ladle him up some mush, and tie on his bib, and pour some molasses over his cereal. I give him his mug of warm milk, and he begins feeding himself. He's just as good as gold.

"Water was frozen, too," says Nathan, " 'bout an inch thick. But I broke the ice with the iron rim of the sweep bucket. It's a clear, cold December morning, sister. Just right for a little walk in the snow. You want to come with me and Little Joe?"

"Come with you where, Nathan?"

"We're walking over to the churchyard. I got to pay my respects to Ma, and visit with her some."

"It's cold for the baby," I say, ladling up mush for the two of us.

"I'll wrap him up snug, in my tippet," says Nathan, "and I'll carry him piggyback."

"Hoss-ee!" says Little Joe.

"That's right!" says Nathan.

"What you got to tell Ma?" I say.

"Oh, there's a power a things I got to say," says Nathan. "Just a power of things she'd want to know."

(29)

"I believe you, Nathan," I say, "and I'd be proud to come along, certain."

"One thing . . . I never *did* tell her about my picture," says Nathan.

"Picture?" I say. "You never told me, neither."

"Well, Joanna," says he, "last July, down in New London, right after I was tendered my lieutenant's commission in the Continental army, a fellow down there painted a miniature of me, in my new uniform. On ivory. And I kept it, since, because I had nobody in particular to give it to."

"Can I see it."

"Certain sure," says Nathan, and he pulls something out of his coat pocket. And he hands me a little silver case, oval shaped, strung on a blue ribbon. A silver locket.

"Snap it open, Joanna," he says. "Just press that button."

The case flies open, and there's Nathan in his soldier's uniform. The same blond hair, the same broad shoulders, the same blue eyes, the same smile.

"It's a good likeness, Nathan," I say. "Looks just like you. Who you going to give it to?"

Nathan reaches over and snaps it closed, and drops it back in his pocket.

"Curiosity killed the cat, Mistress Joanna," says Nathan, with a kind of half smile. "Besides, it's one of the reasons why I want to talk to Ma."

I know who it's for, without asking. It's for Alicia. He's *always* loved her, and now I expect he wants to marry her. Can't be anyone else. Alicia Adams Ripley's

(30)

going to be Mrs. Captain Nathan Hale, if she'll have him. But so soon after her baby's death, and all, I wonder if she will?

We've finished breakfast, so I say, "Nathan, I'm ready to go over to the graveyard anytime you're a mind to."

The three of us bundle up warm, and off we go. It's a mile or so to the churchyard, around the shore of Lake Wangumbaug. But the lake is froze tight, and we take a shortcut across it, and we step along brisk, and we're soon there.

There's the tall white steeple, and beside it, the parson's manse, where Reverend Joseph Huntington taught Nathan and Enoch all the Latin they knew, before they went off to Yale together, better than six years ago. There's white drifts on the windowledges and copings of the manse and the meetinghouse, and the shadowy green branches of the larches sag earthward under heavy loads of snow.

When we get to Ma's grave, Nathan stands there, quiet, looking down at the gentle mound, all blanketed in white. Off in the distance, the sun is glittering on the icy lake.

"It's going to be nine years Ma's dead," says Nathan, "come this April."

"April twenty-first," I say.

"April," says Little Joe.

Ma's grave has a little gray granite marker. The top is rounded, and today it's crowned with a curving ridge of snow. And there's snow in all the designs and crevices where the words are cut into the stone:

IN MEMORY OF
MRS. ELIZABETH
HALE, CONSORT TO
DEACON RICHARD
HALE. DAUGHTER TO
ESQ. JOSEPH AND
MRS. ELIZABETH
STRONG, WHO DIED
APRIL YE 21ST
1767 IN YE 40TH
YEAR OF HER AGE.

And then, nestling beside Ma on the right and left are the two little unmarked graves. That's Jonathan's. He was David's twin brother, though he only lived a week, poor baby. And beside him is Susanna. She was the last of us twelve children, and only lived a month, from February to March, in that same cold winter Ma died.

Nathan hands Little Joe to me, and kneels right down in the snow, beside Ma's grave. He starts right in.

"I've come to tell you, Ma," says Nathan, "about the bright particular star I mean to wed. . . ."

And then he drops his voice low. I know he don't want me to hear the rest. But I'm sure he's telling Ma about Alicia, and nobody else.

I make a snowball for Little Joe. He catches it, and throws it back to me. Nathan gets up out of the snow and lays his hand on the stone for a minute. Then he brushes off his knees and smiles.

"Come on, boy," he says to Little Joe. "Let's play hoss-ee!"

"Hoss-ee!" says Little Joe, holding onto Nathan's neck, and kicking his baby heels.

Nathan jogs up and down some, to make Little Joe laugh. By now the sun's well up above the trees, falling bright yellow on the drifts. Icicles sparkle on the branches, and the blue shadows of naked oaks and elms and hickories cut across our path.

"Joanna," says Nathan, "you won't say anything to anybody, to home, now, will you? Promise me you won't."

"Say anything about what?"

"About the locket."

"I promise."

"I'm thinking to wed," says Nathan, kind of slow, "but I don't know the lady's mind, yet."

"You don't have to speak of it any further to me, Nathan. I know what you're trying to tell me, without any more jabber."

He smiles at me kind of grateful. And we walk across the frozen lake, and the rest of the way back home in silence. And I expect Nathan spent all of that time thinking about his bright particular star.

Nathan gets up early in the morning every day of God's world. And I always get up with the sun, myself. So while he's home on leave, we do most all of our visiting early in the morning, before Pa and Alicia and them are awake.

He likes to talk about liberty and being free from British tyranny, and how General Washington is a hero, and how King George III is a foolish, stubborn tyrant, same as some of the old Greek and Roman tyrants you can read about in Plutarch's *Lives*.

(33)

He likes me to read books aloud with him, too, to improve my spelling and pronunciation and vocabulary.

"Young females," says Nathan, with a grin, "have every bit as much right to the delights of the life of reason as their male counterparts."

He means it, too. Every pretty young lady in Haddam used to get up before five o'clock in the morning to go to his all-female reading classes, before regular classes began, two, three years ago when he was schoolmaster down there.

But I wonder what Pa and Enoch would say if they knew Nathan was reading a stage play with me? Pa says plays are works of Satan and anyone who writes them is reprobate and unregenerate. And yet, Nathan says some of them are all right. He says Mr. Joseph Addison's *Cato* is a fine, enlightened work, perfectly fit for a young lady to read, a noble tragedy, written in an elevated style, and a remarkable model for manly courage. So, he's been having me read it with him, mornings, for a half-hour each day. We're almost finished.

It's about an old Roman—Cato of Utica—who believed Julius Caesar was a tyrant, and fought against him, and lost, and had to kill himself to escape being arrested and executed by Caesar's men.

Nathan has read it many, many times, and he says it is lofty and stirring. I find most of it hard to say, and long, and not very easy to understand. But I like Marcia and Juba. Juba's the black king of Numidia, Cato's ally, and he's in love with Cato's daughter, Marcia. I learned the part where Juba says:

The virtuous Marcia towers above her sex:
True, she is fair (oh, how divinely fair!)
But still the lovely maid improves her charms
With inward greatness, unaffected wisdom,
And sanctity of manners. Cato's soul
Shines out in everything she acts or speaks,
While winning mildness and attractive smiles
Dwell in her looks, and with becoming grace
Soften the rigor of her father's virtues.

That's the way I hope *I'll* be, some day. Like Marcia. Almost as good as my pa, Deacon Richard Hale, maybe. But not quite so stern.

There's another part where Marcia thinks Juba's dead, then learns that he's still alive. She says:

Believe me, prince, before I thought thee dead,
I did not know myself how much I loved thee.

And Juba says:

I'm lost in ecstasy! and dost thou love,
Thou charming maid?

And Marcia answers:

And dost thou live to ask it?

But Nathan brushes over those parts in a hurry, and has me copy out the speeches he likes best, about liberty and resistance to tyranny. And there's plenty of *them.* Here's Cato saying:

A day, an hour, of virtuous liberty
Is worth a whole eternity of bondage.

(35)

and in another place:

> . . . *Valor soars above*
> *What the world calls misfortune and affliction.*

Then Cato says this, about liberty, when his dead son's body is brought to him, and Nathan asked me to copy it out, as well:

> *How beautiful is death, when earned by virtue!*
> *Who would not be that youth? what pity is it*
> *That we can die but once to serve our country!*

And then I copied this part out, too, because Nathan loves it so:

> *We'll sacrifice to liberty.*
> *Remember, O my friends, the laws, the rights,*
> *The generous plan of power delivered down,*
> *From age to age from your renowned forefathers,*
> *(So dearly bought, the price of so much blood)*
> *Oh let it never perish in your hands!*
> *But piously transmit it to your children.*
> *Do thou, great Liberty, inspire our souls,*
> *And make our lives in thy possession happy,*
> *Or our deaths glorious in thy just defense.*

But I hate to think of old Cato and his son dying for liberty, way back then, in Rome. Or us, today, with King George's soldiers shut up inside of Boston by *our* soldiers, with a terrible lot of suffering and dying, maybe, ahead of us all.

As the days of Nathan's furlough pass away, I become more and more sensible of the difficulties the menfolk in this house are having, trying to find sufficient time for private talks with Captain Hale. Pa and Dr. Sam Rose and Enoch are always eager to engage in conversation of a martial character, about the two armies up to Boston, and what the king and the Parliament in London are scheming to do to us rebellious Americans in the colonies. But they can't seem to draw Nathan out, much. Sometimes I see him reading aloud, from that play, *Cato*, to Alicia. Or else he and she go walking in the snow.

Of course, all the womenfolk know what's happening, even though I keep very quiet about the locket he showed me. But the men don't seem to suspect a *thing*. I feel sorriest of all for David. He's just fourteen, and he wants to hear about soldiering, in the worst way— but he can hardly get a word out of Nathan about the camp at Winter Hill, or the siege of Boston. No matter how hard he tries.

Nathan is modest about his soldiering. Almost shy. Tonight, at suppertime, Pa says: "Seems I hear more of your life in service from other folks, Nathan, than I hear from your own lips."

"What do you mean, Father?" says Nathan.

"Well, now," says Pa, "last Sunday, after meeting, Dr. Huntington give me a mighty fine compliment about you. He'd heard from Dr. Munson, in New Haven, that last summer, time you was fixing to quit schoolmastering and begin soldiering, you was quoting Latin verses containing the loftiest kind of patriotic sentiments. Words from Horace. '*Decorum est pro patria mori.*' "

(37)

" '*Dulce et decorum est pro patria mori,*' " said Nathan, blushing. "Well, I own I said it, Father. But 'twas a braggart's remark, spoken heedlessly in the enthusiasm of enlistment. Since then, I been planning to contrive to *live* to a ripe old age."

"Tell me about this decorum poetry foolishness, Nathan," says Grandmother Strong. "What does the Latin mean?"

" 'Sweet and fitting it is,' " says Enoch, " 'to die for your native land.' "

"Lord have mercy!" says Grandmother Strong. "God forbid it should ever come to pass, to any one of you boys!"

"I'll be prudent, Grandma'am," says Nathan.

Then in no time, Mother Abigail breaks in, and we're talking about pleasanter things. But those Latin words—and all of Cato's talk of dying for liberty—leave a dark shadow in the back of my mind.

Nathan can't spend his whole furlough with us, of course. He has to go down to Norwich and New London for a week or two, recruiting new soldiers for Washington's army, and trying to get some of the men who have quit to sign up for another hitch. He rides off, jaunty as can be, on Pa's black stallion, Arab.

While he's gone, Sister Elizabeth Rose and Sarah and Alicia and me keep on with our knitting—wool mittens and stockings—for him to take back to camp in Cambridge.

I can't tell if Nathan has said anything particular to

(38)

Alicia. She never lets on. If he'd give her his locket, I think I'd a known it. But I can't be positive.

The third week in January, Nathan is back with us for a few days. And then, before we know it, we're sitting down to supper and it's his last night together with all of us, before he has to start back to Boston, and camp, early next morning.

Grandmother Strong has baked pumpkin pies from the dried slices of pumpkin Mother Abigail and I set by last fall. And she's boiled a ham, and stuffed and roasted three fat hens. I churned some fresh butter. And there's onions and carrots and parsnips and pickles, fresh bread and apple butter, too. So we have a great plenty, and Nathan and all of us enjoy it.

Nathan sees a parcel of long faces staring at him, around the trestle table, nevertheless. And he's determined to tell a funny story to make things cheery and pleasant for all of us.

"I calculate," says Nathan, smiling real broad, "everybody here has seen the new black and white pictures? The ones that show the profile in black, on a white background? You know what I mean, Sister Rose? They occupy the dizziest pinnacle of fashion here, on this side of the Atlantic, now. Though they've been in high regard, for ten or fifteen years, easy, in France, I'm told."

"Many of us have seen the pictures to which you refer, Captain Hale," says Alicia, real pert, "in the fine houses of Providence, New London, and New Haven.

I dare say they've begun to come into vogue in Boston, as well. We call them silhouettes."

"And if they be *French*, I'll hear no more of them!" says Pa, thumping the table with the flat of his hand. "Didn't your older brothers and I march north to Ticonderoga and Crown Point and Quebec, to drive the unregenerate and reprobate French from Canada? Trying to secure this land, once and for all, for an ungrateful British sovereign? You were only a child of three or four, at the time, Nathan. No doubt, you cannot remember. But I desire to hear nothing more of the French, in this house. Neither in this life, nor in the life to come!"

"Well now, Father," says Nathan, trying to sooth him, "the French may help us yet. And that's part of my little story, if I may tell it."

"Oh, Richard," says Mother Abigail, "let the boy tell his story about the newfangled silhouettes. The French are long gone from Canada—since you chased them thence in 'Fifty-Nine."

"Silhouettes!" growls Pa, and helps himself to the gravy.

"It's well known," says Nathan, "that the whole French nation been hating the British harder than ever, since they lost Canada—as well as India—to the redcoats, back in 'Fifty-Nine, at the end of the French and Indian Wars. And now, to even the score with England, France just *might* help us American rebels in our quarrel with the tyrannous King George III. Some say, indeed, that France is *already* helping us, in secret. But I mustn't speculate upon diplomatic secrets, to which I've no access, nor any certain knowledge. I just want to tell you how these silhouettes came to get their name."

"Well, don't you mind your pa, Nathan," says Grandma'am. "You just *tell* us, no matter what."

"It seems," says Nathan, "that France lost so much money fighting England, she was close to bankrupt. So, King Louis appointed himself a very parsimonious Minister of Finance. And this new minister of the king's tried to convince everybody—even the rich Parisians—that austerities and savings of every kind, skimpy coats and wooden snuffboxes, were going to be regarded henceforth as high fashion."

"Now, that is *uncommon* interesting," says Mother Abigail. "And what was the name of this prudent soul?"

"Why, Mother Abigail," says Nathan, "that fellow's name was Etienne de Silhouette."

"I still don't understand," says Grandmother Strong, "how the pictures come to be called by this foreigner's name."

"The French are a witty and satirical race, Grandma'am," says Nathan. "And they love to mock their politicians. So when Monsieur de Silhouette introduced all these saving ways, the French took to naming his economies after him. They spoke of everything that was saving, or skimpy, or penny-pinching—they spoke of all such economies as being achieved *à la silhouette*. That is to say: in the manner in which Monsieur de Silhouette would like to see it done. And so, when these black and white profiles were invented, in Paris, the French joked, and said that Monsieur de Silhouette was *bound* to approve of them, because they were sure to be much cheaper than portraits painted in oils. And they

(41)

called them portraits fashioned *à la silhouette*. And finally, just plain silhouettes!"

That seems so comical that all of us have a good laugh.

"And how do folks make these silhouettes?" says David.

"In a dark room," says Nathan, "with a dark lantern, the door opened just a crack. Then you put up some white paper, on the wall, and trace around the outline of the shadow of your profile. And there's your portrait, *à la silhouette*!"

"I admit it's comical," says Pa. "But it's still too French for me."

"Well, it ain't too French for *me*!" says Mother Abigail. "I believe I'd like to have me a silhouette of this old phiz—that old reprobate and unregenerate French King Louis notwithstanding."

"There's a girl of spirit, Abby!" says Grandmother Strong. "I've a mind to see my silhouette, too!"

"And I," says Sally.

"And I," says Sister Rose.

"And I," says I.

"And I, too, should find it most diverting," says Alicia Ripley, looking sidewise at Nathan.

"Well, Father," laughs Dr. Sam Rose, "all your womenfolk have banded together against ye. Such female solidarity cannot be gainsayed. I expect we men must make the best of it we can, and let these weaker vessels have their headstrong way."

"I ain't going to join you," says Pa, getting up from the table. "But I ain't going to be the spoil-sport,

(42)

neither. The rest of you do what you want to do, and make yourselves merry."

There's a dark lantern up in Nathan's room, up in the north chamber. So all of us troop upstairs. And we have us a time, giggling in the dark, while first Grandmother Strong, then Mother Abigail, then Sarah, then Sister Rose, then Alicia, then me, have us a silhouette drawn on a sheet of paper, by Nathan, while David works the lantern. Pretty soon we've used up the few sheets of paper we have. Of course, Pa and Dr. Sam and Enoch are too grave and serious-minded to consider letting us make silhouettes of *them*. But I know what I'm after.

"Now, you oblige me, Nathan," I say. "I want to make me a silhouette of *you*. And I'm not joking, neither."

"All right, Joanna," he says. "I don't mind."

We have no paper left, so I stand Nathan up, in the middle of the chamber, and David cracks open the dark lantern, and—with a big black pencil, on the chamber door—I trace out this drawing of Nathan's forehead and eyebrow and nose and lips and chin, just as careful as can be. He turns his head just a bit, to watch what I'm doing, so it ain't a full profile, quite. But everybody says it looks just like Nathan. Except Alicia. And she says nothing at all.

When we're all back downstairs again, Nathan remembers what he has to do. "I mustn't let this evening slip past," says he, "without stepping over to Asher Wright's place. He promised me an answer, before I left for camp."

(43)

"Well, now," says Pa, "I'm hoping Asher may see fit to do his duty by General Washington. And I can appreciate that a captain like you needs someone up to camp to prepare his meals and wait on him, and all. Even though I had been calculating to have Asher and everyone over here, come spring, to help me put up the frame of the new house, soon as the frost was out of the ground."

"I'll give you his answer, Father," says Nathan, "before I leave in the morning."

Nathan and Alicia stand murmuring in the shadows by the back door for a moment or two. Then Nathan takes his cloak and lantern, and strides off alone, to fetch his answer from Asher.

Tonight, Sister Rose let me have Little Joe with me in my room, in the southwest chamber. If it weren't for that, and the thunderstorm, I would never have known how it is, between Alicia and Nathan.

Long before Nathan came back from Asher Wright's place, all of us said good-night, and started up to bed. Each of us with a candle, flickering in its pewter holder. I set my candle down on the stand beside my pillow, and bent down to look at Little Joe. He was asleep, in his trundle bed, with a red and blue quilt pulled up under his fat, pink little chin.

No sooner am I in my nightdress than Grandmother Strong raps on the wall, from next door.

"Joanna!" she whispers. "Joanna, come here."

In I go, and there's Grandma'am in her white wool wrapper and her big, pumpkin-shaped night cap, sitting on the edge of her big four-poster bed.

(44)

"Pet," she says, as urgent as may be, "I must trouble you to go down to the kitchen hearth, for hot coals. I'll have my death of cold if I put these old bones into that icy vastness." And I know she means the sheets are too cold and damp for her.

"It's no trouble, Grandma'am," I say, and I mean it. Nothing is too much trouble if Grandmother Strong needs my help. I go down, get the bed-warmer, and fill it with coals. Then I climb the stairs and warm the sheets. And we kiss each other good-night.

"Wake me up in the morning, before Nathan leaves," she says, and I say yes, and shut the door.

In a moment I'm in my own bed and I hear Little Joe breathing peacefully beside me. It's pitch dark outside, with no trace of a moon. I say my prayers, and then I suppose I drop off to sleep in no time, as I always do.

What seems to be moments later, the baby is crying. Screaming in terror. The wind is whistling and what must be hail is beating on the roof and on the window-panes. There's a flash of lightning and then such a terrible thunderclap that the house shakes—rocking and swaying, it seems like, under my bed.

"There, there, there . . ." I say, to the baby. I pick him up and put him on my shoulder and try to comfort him. He stops crying as soon as I touch him. But as I walk over to the trundle bed to put him down again, I see a crack of light under the door.

I step out into the hall with the baby on my shoulder. It must be long past midnight. But there is Alicia, with her black cloak thrown over her nightgown, and a candle in her hand. There's something in her other

(45)

hand that she's studying. It's hanging from around her neck, on a thin blue ribbon. She's standing in the door of Nathan's bedchamber, looking from whatever she's holding in her hand, up to the silhouette of his face that I drew this evening. Up and back again to something she's holding in her hand.

"Alicia," I say.

She cries out, real sharp and startled, and drops the candle. We're left in darkness.

"What's the matter?" I say. "It's only me. Joanna."

"Nathan," she says. "Nathan's gone. . . ."

There's lightning again, and I can see his bed, untouched, in the momentary flash.

"He must still be over to Asher's, Alicia," I say. "You remember he said he was trying to recruit Asher for a soldier."

"I know. I know," says Alicia. And I hear her voice real close to tears. "It's just that I was worried about his going, tomorrow. And the storm woke me, and. . . ."

The lightning comes again, and I can see what she's holding in her hand. It's the oval miniature, in the little silver case. Nathan, with his blond hair, and his blue eyes laughing out, and his fine, firm mouth just smiling, smiling. . . .

I believe Alicia must have stayed up half the night, waiting for Nathan to come back from Asher Wright's. We couldn't arouse her this morning, I know. And Nathan had his breakfast and was long gone before she awoke.

(46)

But I arise before sun-up, and so does Grandmother Strong, and Pa, and Sarah, and Enoch, and David, and Mother Abigail, and Sister Rose and Little Joe. All of us try to pretend that it's like any other day. Nathan drinks his hot rum and eats his fried eggs and bacon, and we brush off his blue uniform and bundle him up in his greatcoat and boots and tie his hat down with a long wool scarf, and tell him to be prudent, and to let some of the Massachusetts boys do their share of the fighting, too, 'long of him.

He's got the socks and the mittens Sister Rose and I been knitting for him, in his pocket. Just before he leaves he turns to Grandmother Strong and says, "Grandma'am, I hope you'll think to send me some Holland linen, for shirts, this spring. And some linsey-woolsey britches, come fall."

Then he shakes hands, good-bye, to Father and Dr. Sam and Enoch and David.

"Asher Wright's going to enlist, Father," says he. "He told me last night. He'll be leaving with me, this morning."

Nathan lifts Little Joe way up in the air and hollers "Hoss-eeeee!" And he kisses Grandma'am, and Mother Abigail, and Sarah, and Sister Rose.

When he hugs and kisses me good-bye his whiskers scratch my face, and I say, "Nathan, now you be careful!" And he crushes me real tight up against all those metal buttons on the front of his uniform.

Then he says, "Don't you let that baby forget his Uncle Nathan!" And he tramps through the snow to the barn, saddles up Arab, and trots across the fields to meet Asher. And he's gone.

(47)

PART TWO

Twenty-five Yards of Linen

I CAN FEEL SPRING BEGINNING to thaw the winter and soften the air, even though we're still in February. Pa says it was a thawing night, last night, even though the northwest wind is still cold. And now today is sunny and warm, so he allows the sugar maples are beginning to flow. The tips of the branches have been carrying their buds already formed, ever since last fall. They haven't begun to swell or to turn red yet, far as I can see. But if Pa says the maples have begun to flow, I calculate it's so. He knows a world of things about this farm.

Pa says that the Lord God Jehovah has arranged for the sugar maples to flow more by day, and to ease up during the night. The sap sometimes rises faster on the south side of the tree. And on the east side, too, Pa told me last night at supper. He says he's seen the flow stop dead when the wind veers 'round to the southwest, or whenever there's a threat of a storm.

But today the wind is right and the sky is clear. So this afternoon maybe he'll tap some trees, and let me come along. I've been waiting for spring all this dreary winter through. And now it's maple sugaring time at last.

I can't think of maple sugar without thinking of Nathan. It's almost a month since he went back to

Cambridge, just outside of Boston, back to his camp on Winter Hill. He told Alicia they named it Winter Hill, a while back, because all the soldiers' white canvas tents, pitched there, made the hillside look like it was covered with snow. And now with all this sharp winter weather, I expect he's had his fill of real snow, certain sure.

We have. When I look out my chamber window, there's pale yellow sunlight glittering on the snowy branches of the big pear tree, and a cold snowy carpet over the fields. I tire of sitting here at my spinning wheel, listening to the low, droning hum of the wheel turning, the clack of the treadle, and the squeak of the spools. There's a tan bundle of flax tied to the distaff— the long upstanding rod that Grandmother Strong calls "the rock," the way the old people do. That big hank of flax tied up there on my distaff looks just like old Mr. Nathaniel Wright's head, when he permits his hair to blow about uncombed. He's Asher's father.

That makes me think of Asher and Nathan, all over again, at Winter Hill. My wheel slows and stops, and soon I'm staring out at the snow on the roof of the barn. The room grows still.

"Joanna," Mother Abigail calls. "Let me hear that wheel a-humming. Less you can be more industrious than *that*, you won't have near enough thread for your warp. And then what will you say to Grandmother Strong?"

Of course, Mother's right. I sigh and start my wheel again. Its dismal whining and groaning fill the room once more. My fingers are red and smarting from the

(52)

fibers of the line. That's what Grandmother Strong calls the nice long, even flax fibers—"the line." The few little broken pieces I failed to comb out—the ones that aren't good for much because they won't twist up into a fine long thread—the little pieces are called "the tow." Grandma'am says we must even save the tow, this year, and make good use of it for coarse cloth. But we're using only the best of the line for Nathan's Holland. He'll need some linen shirts for summer, and Grandma'am says it's past time she taught me how to throw the shuttle on her loom, over to her place.

I miss seeing Grandma'am every day, since she moved back to her own home, just down the road. We had her with us while Nathan and Brother Joseph were here on furlough. But when their visits was over, Grandma'am moved back home, to get her own work done.

"Hale and Strong!" she says, with a laugh. "That's what all you children are! Hale and Strong!" That's a little family saying she has, for jollity's sake. I mean, when Sarah and Alicia and Mother Abigail aren't present. 'Twas my *own* Mother's name, Strong was, before she married Pa. While Mother Abigail's maiden name was Cobb, 'fore she married Captain Sam Adams, first, and after she was a widow, Pa.

Mother Abigail is a good mother, too, even though she never was a Strong. And there aren't any of us children don't love her, and Sarah, and Alicia, too, same as all the rest of our own full kin.

I'll never stop grieving for Ma, though. And wishing she was still here to help us, with all there is to do. There'd be work enough for Pa and all of us, building a great new house with two chimneys, and running this big farm, even if all eight of my brothers was still with us here to home. Wouldn't Ma have loved this new house we're to have, I'm thinking?

But six of my brothers are off fighting the British. And that don't leave but Brother Enoch and young David to help Pa with the stone and the timbers and digging the cellar hole and all the ploughing! Pa says he'll have to hire more help. There's no other way. Brother David gets taller and stronger every day, of course, but he isn't yet fourteen.

Pa says we shall overcome all our tribulations with the assistance of the wonder-working providence of the Lord God Jehovah. And to that, all we women can say nothing but Amen!

But I do wish my own ma could be here to see all of us now, bustling about as we are, striving for *both* worlds, as Reverend Huntington says.

This very morning, Pa is down back, behind the barn, cleaning out the lambing shed, to make it dry and sweet. Three black-faced ewes have dropped their lambs last night, and Pa and Brother David was up, by lantern light, seeing to them. There'll be thirty more of them—new born and frisking and bleating—before the month is out. When my spinning's done, I must go out back to see them, nuzzling their mothers. Pa feeds them crushed-up linseed cakes, and oats, soon's they're old enough to eat solid food. And while they're nursing, we feed the ewes kale and turnips, as well as hay, to help them have plenty of milk for their lambs.

Mother Abigail is downstairs, bent over her quilting frame, padding a quilt in the double wedding ring pattern. Sister Sally is in the next room, thumping at the loom. I can hear her beater smacking the woolen weft, while she's weaving linsey-woolsey, inch by inch. Alicia's in there with her, turning out yarn on the big wheeled spinning wheel—the one we use for wool. I have the little wheel up here in the bedroom with me— the one we use for flax.

I'd be down there with them if I didn't have my reading to do—for I can't read with Mother and Sally and Alice talking between the rooms.

Trust Pa to think of every way to strike out at "profligate Britannia," as he calls the royal government in London. Other day a recruit come up the road, on his way to camp. Pa had him in and fed him, as he always does with any soldier he sees passing by. And after a time, he sees the soldier watching Sister Alice at her spinning.

"Now, sergeant," says Pa, "don't you go conceiving that that woolen yarn is intended to warm the useless backsides of any of us farm folk, here to home. Every ell, every yard, every *inch* of any woolens spun and woven here goes direct to the soldiers in the province of Massachusetts, in the Continental Army!"

The sergeant laughed, but Pa meant every word.

Mother Abigail said, after the soldier went on his way, he most likely wasn't speculating about yarn at all. He was probably just admiring Alicia. And Pa said that was a lamentable and light-minded observation, and he never wanted to hear nothing to equal it again. Pa can be something stern.

(55)

Nathan conjured me, before he left, to be a good little scholar, all on my own, whilst he's away. And I promised him I'd try to keep up with my reading. But try and find time for reading on this farm!

So, I've tied my little book up on the distaff of my spinning wheel, just below the hank of flax, so's I can work and read all at once. Otherwise, I don't know when there'd be time for improving my mind.

It's a new pamphlet I'm studying, printed just last month in Philadelphia. Reverend Huntington lent it to us, for Brother Enoch to read, but he's finished it, now. Everybody hereabouts is talking about it. Reverend Huntington read out parts of it from the pulpit this past Sunday, at meeting. And Brother Enoch read some of it aloud to us, this week, in the evening, after supper.

Many's the man stops wavering in his mind, once he's read it, and says, "By the great gun bullets! He's hit it square on the head! It's *time* to part!"

I will not say I find it easy to comprehend in all its pages, and I stumble over a nation of the longer words. But I can understand this writer's drift. For he can't *abide* kings, and neither can I. He writes:

. . . . Of more honest worth is one honest man to society, and in the sight of God, than all the crowned ruffians that ever lived.

Well, I'm of his mind there! I think my father, or Brother Nathan, are bound to be worth more than that red-faced old King George, with all his tantrums! He *may* be a "ruffian," too, as this fellow writes. I have to stop now and then to turn a page, and prop my book back up, just so. They say it's written by a Mr. Thomas Paine, and very persuasive he can be. He calls it *Common Sense*. Listen to him, here, talking about a train of events very dear to my Yankee heart:

> . . . let our imaginations transport us a few moments to Boston; that seat of wretchedness will teach us wisdom, and instruct us forever to renounce a power in whom we can have no trust. The inhabitants of that unfortunate city, who but a few months ago were in ease and affluence, have now no other alternative than to stay and starve, or turn out to beg. Endangered by the fire of their own friends if they continue within the city, and plundered by the soldiery if they leave it.

Poor besieged Boston! Feeling the linen thread slip through my aching fingers, looking out over the peaceful snowy fields around our quiet house, I begin wondering what it must be like to have to live in a city, with a British army cooped up within, and a Yankee army camped 'round about, outside.

Of course, all this trouble with Parliament and the king has been brewing for about fifteen years, now, Pa says. And I won't be but twelve years old myself, until March 19. So I'm just beginning to understand some part of it, and get a bit of it sorted out in my head. Pa tells it real downright and simple.

He says it cost Britain a world of money to run out the French and Indians, and take possession of Canada, back in '59—even though we Americans did most of the fighting, and a good deal of the footing of the bills, ourselves. Still, when the whole thing was over, in '63, Britain tried to find a way to get us Yankees to pay her back for her trouble and expense. And that's when all the trouble began.

Pa says even before I was born Britain was claiming she had the right to ruin our trade in sugar and molasses from the West Indies. And British soldiers started breaking into merchants' warehouses—without search warrants—to see if they were smuggling, and so on.

Now *that* made us poorer and angrier than we were before—not being able to trade free—and since Britain couldn't collect much money from us, she began trying to put more taxes on us—taxes voted on us over there, in Parliament, in London. *Not* voted by our own assemblies here, the way they always had been. And we said they couldn't *do* that to us! Britain didn't have the right, and we wouldn't allow her to usurp it.

Pa gets angry and stutters when he tells me about it. In '65—when I was just a year and a half—there came the Stamp Act, that tried to put a tax on wills and marriage certificates and other legal documents and newspapers and almanacs.

By the time I was two, in 1766, there'd been so much remonstrance and confusion and protest over the Stamp Act that Britain decided to repeal it, and all the colonies celebrated. Pa says we rang steeple bells, and shot off cannon. And up in Boston they had an "illumination," and everybody put lighted candles in the windows of their houses, to show how happy they were that the trouble had passed away.

But it hadn't passed away for good. Parliament in London was still determined to tax us, one way or another. And a year later, when I was three—the year Ma died—along came the Townshend Acts that put a tax on window glass, and lead for paint, and on paper, and on tea. Pa says everybody quit using glass and paint and paper, and stopped drinking tea, and vowed they wouldn't buy anything else from England, ever again, as long as those taxes remained unjustly fastened to those products.

Then in '68, when I was four, the king sent shiploads of redcoats to Boston, because he suspected that worse trouble was coming. Nobody in Boston wanted his soldiers living in their houses, but they were forced to take them in and board them, anyway.

By the time I was six, came the Boston Massacre, and when I was nearly ten, the Boston Tea Party. I remember *that* myself. It was in December, 1773, when they tried to land the tea ships' cargoes in Boston—all that tea with their new tax on it—and the Sons of Liberty disguised themselves, dressed up like Mohawk Indians, and they dumped the tea in the harbor.

Five or six months after that, King George locked the port of Boston up, tight! Not one ship allowed to sail in or out. He closed it tight as a drum—punishing them for their tea party. And Boston would have *starved* if wagons of food hadn't been sent into the city from thousands of friends round about.

In September of '74, when I was ten and a half, and Nathan had graduated from Yale and started teaching school, the First Continental Congress—with delegates from all the colonies but Georgia—met in Philadelphia, and told the king he didn't have the right to treat free Englishmen the way he was treating us.

Then just last spring, in '75, came the worst trouble of all. Some British troops marched out of Boston, in

April, to take up some muskets and gunpowder that we
Yankee patriots—our Sons of Liberty—had stored in
Concord. And the Yankee minutemen in Lexington
and round about fired on the redcoats, and the shooting
started in earnest. I'll never forget it. Pa says General
Israel Putnam was doing spring plowing, in his fields,
right here in this province of Connecticut, up in Pom-
fret, when he heard the news. Putnam left his plow
right there in the field—didn't even unhitch the team—
and set off, at once, for Boston. Three of my brothers
—Sam, and Sally's husband, John, and Joe—they set
right out for Boston too. Soon there was sixteen thousand Yankees up there, hemming the British in. In
June came the Battle of Bunker Hill. And in July,
General Washington took command. That same
month, Nathan give up teaching school, and got his
army commission as a lieutenant, and he's been up there
ever since.

Now this fellow Thomas Paine is writing that we
must part from Britain, and the king, and make us a
country of our own. There's others saying the same
thing, but not so well as he does, in this pamphlet,
Common Sense:

> The sun never shined on a cause of greater worth. 'Tis
> not the affair of a city, a county, a province, or a kingdom,
> but of a continent—of at least one-eighth part of the habitable
> globe. 'Tis not the concern of a day, a year, or an age;
> posterity are virtually involved in the contest, and will be
> more or less affected, even to the end of time, by the
> proceedings now. Now is the seed time of continental
> union, faith, and honor. The least fracture now will be like

a name engraved with the point of a pin on the tender rind of a young oak; the wound will enlarge with the tree, and posterity read it in full grown characters.

My room is growing warmer as the sun rises higher in the sky. It's almost noon. There is a drip of melting snow from the eaves. Outside, in the crisp morning air, Father and Brother David are sawing timbers for the frame of the new house. I can hear the bite of the ripsaw as it tears its way through a great oaken slab. Father stands down inside the sawpit. Brother David stands above, on the beam that is being divided down its entire length. Brother Enoch is also working and sweating at peaceful pursuits, for there is the steady clop, clop, clop of his adze, as he squares and levels a huge summer beam—for so we call the tremendous main ceiling support which will run through the center of the keeping room.

How far away seem the fifes and drums and musketry of Boston. Can we be at war, I wonder, with the maple trees beginning to flow, and three new spring lambs in the lambing shed, bawling for their mothers' milk? My mother and my sisters' voices hum softly over their sewing and spinning. Over the creak and thump of the loom. The smell of the thick bean soup we shall soon be eating floats up the stairwell. I know there is death and danger threatening. But it seems so distant, this morning, from our peaceful Connecticut farm.

And yet, there's a flash of bayonets glinting up from the pages of the little pamphlet tied onto my distaff.

Here it speaks of "our bleeding country"—the very words that Brother Nathan sometimes uses—and it says:

> Everything that is right or natural pleads for separation. The blood of the slain, the weeping voice of nature cries, *'tis time to part*.
>
> The present winter is worth an age if rightly employed, but if lost or neglected, the whole continent will partake of the misfortune. . . .

I shiver at my spinning, rubbing my sore fingers on my skirts as I read his advice: that we begin at once to build a powerful navy. But what of Britain's fearsome navy? Those tall, cruel frigates that—for all I know—may be slipping into undefended towns along the Connecticut shore of Long Island Sound? And the endless redcoated legions of "the royal brute," King George? How shall we ever overcome so much tyranny and power, and shake ourselves free?

And what will my poor brave brothers do if our rebellion should fail? This little pamphlet of Mr. Paine's is very sure, and very brave. It says that we must stop begging the king for justice, and declare our independence, boldly. But his *pamphlet* don't have to bleed and suffer and die.

I have broken my thread. So now I must mend it, and start up my wheel again, paying better attention to the tautness and pressure of my spinning. For good linen thread has to be tightly twisted, but it must remain lithe and springy, nonetheless.

Mother Abigail calls upstairs, telling me that I must come down soon and set the table for our midday meal.

The clop, clop, clop of Brother Enoch's adze keeps up its steady pace, like the ticking of a giant clock.

And yet I am compelled to turn back to the final pages of my pamphlet. Think of it, Joanna Hale! Such times to be alive in! And such words of fire!

> We have every opportunity to form the noblest, purest constitution on the face of the earth. We have it in our power to begin the world over again. A situation similar to the present hath not happened since the days of Noah until now. The birthday of a new world is at hand. . . .

There! I've broken my thread a second time! And Mother Abigail is calling "Bean soup! Joanna! Bean soup is ready!"

We have it in our power *to begin the world over again!* I'm about dizzy with the thought! And then I think of Noah and all the animals marching two by two into the ark. And then I think of Pa out there half of the night, with the ewes and the lambs. Then I untie the pamphlet and put it back on the desk in Brother Enoch's chamber, where I found it. And I run downstairs for my midday meal.

Enoch and Pa and David have been working so hard this morning they're almost steaming with sweat when they wash off on the back stoop and come on in for their food.

"You get that beam squared up, Enoch?" says Pa.

"Yes, Father," says Enoch, sitting down at the table

(63)

and letting out a sigh. "It's seasoned oak, from the heart of that great tree you felled yourself, over in the north forty last March—just before we got the news of Lexington. It's oak, and it's stout and it's hard."

"Make a mighty good summer beam, then," says Pa.

"No doubt," says Enoch. "It's hard as granite."

"Well, we might's well build to last," says Pa. "House can hold my grandchildren, and *yours*, too, if we build it strong enough. Hewn and braced and pegged to stand up to the trials bound to come."

"Oh, Deacon Hale," says Mother Abigail, "do say grace now, while the bean soup's still smoking hot."

"Almighty God," says Pa, real stern, like he was reproving a farm hand. "We ask for mercy and approbation in Thy sight this day. We're all of us working hard for our own furtherance—here among our neighbors on earth, where we hope to enjoy such bounty as Thou mayest accord us. And we trust and pray for reunion with those we love, at last, through Thy everlasting grace and goodness, in Thy heavenly kingdom, above. Amen."

Then Mother Abigail ladles out the soup from the pot over the fire, and we cut the loaf of bread, and begin.

"It's four more ewes'll be dropping lambs before morning, David," says Pa. "Make sure the lanterns are trimmed afresh with candles. We won't be sleeping overmuch this night, I'll hazard."

"We'll have more than thirty lambs, this year, if all be spared," says Mother Abigail.

"Oh, they'll be spared," says Sister Sally, "if Father Hale is tending them at birth. Though precious little of their wool we'll be using ourselves, while there's a single Continental soldier left to be clad."

"*Precious* little," says Pa. "We won't be using a hank of it for ourselves, this year, Sally."

"Let me sit up and help tonight, with the lambs, instead of David," says Alicia, looking up at Pa.

"It ain't for women to be pestered with flocks and lambing," says Pa. "I thank ye, Alice. But you and Sally and Sister Rose and Joanna best keep helping Mother with the house, here. And we'll do what's to be done out back. Every one of us has more than ample toil in store this spring. Setting in this cellar, and laying the chimneys for the new house. And squaring up beams, and pegging the frames and all. To say nothing of the ploughing and the sowing. We'll be growing more flax this year, along of corn and buckwheat and all the garden greens. There's a *nation* of work for every one of us. Don't you be uneasy you won't come in for your share."

"I was telling Madam Huntington, last Sunday, to meeting," says Mother Abigail, "that I'm to have a fine great house, with a center hall, and a tall staircase, and eight rooms and *two* chimneys, with a fireplace in every room!"

"Finer than the parsonage itself," says Sister Rose, reaching over to wipe some soup from Little Joe's chin.

"And ours only just so long as we may be worthy of it, in the sight of the Lord God Jehovah," says Pa.

"Well, Father," says Brother Enoch. "There's no whirlwind can shake loose the summer beam I been smoothing this morning. It's granite oak to the core."

"It can't be no harder than the framing timbers we

(65)

been sawing in the pit," says David, filling up his bowl with more soup.

"We'll need help from all over, come May or June, when it's time for the raising," says Pa. "I'll talk to Nathan'l Wright this afternoon, about the masonry, and the extra teams of oxen for the stone boats. But you'll have to gather in all the family, and all the neighbors for me, Enoch, when it's time the frame goes up."

"I'll see that they're all here, Father," says Enoch, smiling at Alicia. But Alicia don't seem to notice Enoch hardly at all.

I keep wanting to break in, to tell everyone that "the birthday of a new world is at hand," like the pamphlet said. But I'm only a little girl in their sight, and they might laugh at me. So I don't speak out after all. Not about the pamphlet.

"Is it time to tap the sugar maples, Pa?" I say.

"Well, Joanna," says Pa, "I think it may be. But I'll just ask Nathan'l Wright what he says, to make certain sure. You can step over there, with me, and we'll ask him, after we've hed our soup."

"Oh, I'd *like* that, Pa," I answer. And his eyes kind of twinkle, though his mouth don't seem to be laughing.

Enoch and David and Pa been working so hard all morning they're wolf hungry. They have three bowls of soup apiece. Then Mother Abigail has apple pie and hot cider for us all.

When we're through, Pa says, "Come on, Joanna," and I get my hooded cloak and my pattens for the snow, and my mittens, and off we start for Mr. Wright's.

(66)

Pa and I tramp ac.oss the yard without speaking. The bare trees stand out black against the melting snow. Not a single bud or blade of green is showing. But the sky is blue, and the air is mild and warm, and I can see that the withes on the willow trees that grow along the brook have took on that glowing pinkish brown, the way they do just before they turn their pale yellow-green.

"It smells of spring," I say.

" 'Twon't be spring for a good five, six weeks," says Pa, "though the days are longer, and the season's turned for sure. So it's none too soon for me to firm up my bargain with Nathan'l Wright."

"Before we set off, Pa, may we look at the lambs?"

Pa allows we can, and we go into the big barn where the oxen and cows and the horses are ranged, stomping in their proper stalls. There's three or four pens of sheep, and some hens and geese stalking about, searching for grain.

"There's the four ewes that be due to lamb tonight," says Pa, "and here's the three with their new-born, day old lambs."

I look at the gentle, black-faced sheep. Their winter fleeces are thick. The little lambs, on their wobbly legs, are half hidden under their mothers. They're busy nursing. Their pink skin shows through their wispy, ragged little coats. They seem too tiny to bleat, almost.

"They must be cold," I say to Pa.

"The ewes know how to keep them warm," says Pa. " 'Lamb without blemish and without spot,' " says Pa, "from the First epistle of Peter, chapter one, verse nineteen. They ain't too cold, Joanna."

"I love them. I love *anything* little."

"Mighty becoming, in a young woman," says Pa, as if he were smiling at me. Only he's not.

"The lambs will keep, but my business with Nathan'l Wright will *not*," says Pa, and away we start. I crane my neck around for a last sight of the lambs and ewes.

It only takes us a few minutes to walk through the snow to Mr. Wright's house. He's Asher's father, and Asher's been off to war with Brother Nathan since back in January. The Wrights been neighbors of ours ever since I was born. We help each other out at harvest time, and whenever there's a need.

We find Mr. Wright out back, splitting logs. We don't go inside, though he's hospitable enough and invites us in.

"I come over, Nathan'l," says Pa, "to firm up our compact in regard to your teams of oxen."

"Good a time as any, Deacon," says Mr. Wright, setting his axe and his wedges down on the block, and wiping his brow on his sleeve. "Hev you heard from Nathan since he went back last month? We ain't heard no word from Asher."

"Nathan don't write too frequent," says Pa. "But I'll be sure to read you his next letter, should he mention Asher."

"His mother mourns him, as if he were dead for sure," says Mr. Wright.

"Women," says Pa.

Mr. Wright nods.

"Can I ask about the sugaring off, Pa?" says I.

"Waal, now, Joanna," says Mr. Wright. "You must have the least tetch of the second sight in you, just as

I do. This is a sap-running day, for certain. But I'm always the fust around here to know. And here *you* know it, too!"

"I just had a feeling," says I.

"I was out this morning to my big grove—you know, the big sugar bush on the hill where my best stand of stone maples be," says Mr. Wright. "Out there this morning with two of my boys. Took along our bit and auger, and bored thirty, forty trees. Knocked the spigots in and hung the buckets. We be b'iling us some maple sap by the end of this week. Saturday, I expect. You and David come on by, and bring young little Master Joe Rose, too. Hev you some maple syrup poured over a bowl of snow!"

"Thank you, Mr. Wright. We'll be there, certain," I say.

And Pa says, "About them oxen. . . ."

"Now, Deacon," says Mr. Wright. "I give you my word as my bond, back in December, I'd be harnessing up them evil-tempered brutes, chaining them fast to my stone boats. And I promised you I'd be at your disposal this spring, soon's the frost was out of the ground. Ready to haul stone for you, direct from the quarry. And you agreed to pay me two shillings a week for the labor. And I'm as good as my word, and as soon as the thaw is upon us, I'll be there with my teams."

"By the great gun bullets, Nathan'l!" says Pa, "don't be sharp with me! You've never yet gone back on your word, nor was I suggesting you were about to."

"Deacon," says Mr. Wright, somewhat more peaceful in his manner, "if there's one thing I know, it's stone. Granite. Quarrying. There sap in stone, Deacon. Same as there is in maple trees. Nobody's going to try to cut no stone for ye, while the ground water's all froze. Stone has to be wet—sopping wet. Filled with water. Filled with sap, or won't no worthwhile mason touch it. Cuts better that way. Easier. Truer. I *know* about them big chimney piers you need, and that long wall of dressed stone you're aiming to build around the kitchen garden. But you won't be heving no stone cut for it before March fifteenth, I vow, or my name ain't Nathan'l Wright! The sap be froze up tight in the granite till then. You'll see. And my masons won't *touch* it till it's wet."

"I understand, Brother Wright," says Pa, kind of weary and patient. "I'd just thought I better assure myself you'd not forgot our engagement."

"Forgot!" says Mr. Wright, real indignant, rearing up like a bantam rooster. His blue eyes glint, and he shakes his head and tousels his hair. It looks just like the flax on my distaff back home. "I forget no engagements with Deacon Hale," says he. "I make a bargain, and I hold to it!"

"Indeed, you always hev, Brother Wright," says Pa.

"Always hev, and always will," says Mr. Wright. "But look here, why are we jabbering out here, in the snow? Don't you want to step inside the barn and see my new team?"

"I'd be proud to, Nathan'l," says Pa. " 'The ox knoweth his owner, and the ass his master's crib.' "

"Scripture?" says Mr. Wright, looking real shrewd at Pa.

"Scripture," says Pa. "First chapter Isaiah, third verse."

(70)

Mr. Wright ain't certain Pa's joking with him, but *I'm* sure he is. There's nobody more quick-witted than Pa, and I've got the hang of his joking, at last. Sly.

"Well, sir," says Mr. Wright, throwing open his barn doors, "these be some of the daintiest looking red oxen I ever clapped eye on. Cream-spotted, and strong enough to uproot a grove of oak, if I was to whup 'em hard enough."

"You'll not whip these beasts, whilst you're using them in *my* employ," says Pa. "I don't hold with cruelty to patient creatures. Never did."

I stand looking at the oxen, staring at their muscled haunches, and their huge forequarters. They have iron rings in their noses, and their horns clack against the worn slats of their stanchions. They low and bellow over their hay. All twelve of them are powerful. The old team are dun-colored, with black feet and tails. But the new teams are as glossy and as red-brown as chestnuts, with creamy faces and throats and feet. They all stand a good six inches higher than the duns.

"They're beauties, Nathan'l," says Pa.

"Not altogether," says Mr. Wright, with a laugh. "Now, I will say they be a Yankee-good team of oxen, but still, they got names that fit their dispositions close. Names signifying that they be a sight more unregenerate in their inward spirit, than my patient team of duns."

"What are their names?" say I.

"Well, Joanna," says Mr. Wright, "you remember the names of some of my old team, I expect? This here's Perseverance, and then there's Chastity, and Righteous Endeavor—him with the crumpled horn. And the other three duns is Faith, Hope, and Charity."

(71)

"I remember," I say.

"A virtuous lot," says Pa, with a smile. "But what about the team of reds?"

"A different case, Deacon," says Mr. Wright. "A very different case, indeed. A wicked, bad-tempered lot. They need the goad and the lash, beauties though they may be."

"But what are their *names*, Brother!" says Pa, snorting real impatient.

"Their names," says Mr. Wright, "will doubtless fail to please ye. For this here's Reprobate. And this is Papist. And these two, Fire and Brimstone. And this great fellow's Sin. And here, with the big black hooves and snout, this here's Satan!"

"A fantastical and self-indulgent nomenclature!" says Pa, screwing up his mouth to keep from laughing. "And still I say, Nathan'l, you'll not be welcome to lash at Sin and Satan while you're hauling stone for me! I'll expect temperance and kind words to prevail while you're driving the reds, same as when you're handling the virtuous duns. And no whips at all. Agreed?"

"Deacon Hale! Deacon Hale!" says Mr. Wright. "How can I hope to flout the wishes of a man as mild and godly as yourself? *Without* whips, then, as you insist. Though the work may take a nation longer, under your conditions. But this I'll tell you. *Nobody* gets Nathan'l Wright to the quarry until March, when the thaw's upon us, and the granite's full of sap!"

"The point's well made and well taken, Nathan'l," says Pa. "We'll expect you and your sledges and your oxen, time we get a thaw."

"And I'll expect you and anyone wants to come, over

to the sugar bush, come this Saturday, for the sap-b'iling, and a maple sugar feast."

Then Pa and me leave the great beasts lowing around him, in his barn, and we trudge our way back home through the mushy snow.

The next morning after my visit to Mr. Wright's with Pa, the weather holds warm and the sky is fair. Since the wind hasn't veered, I calculate the sap has kept on running in the maples.

It's the Sabbath, and we all drive into South Coventry, to meeting. All of us, in the farm wagon, together: Grandmother Strong, Dr. Sam and Sister Rose and Little Joe, and all the rest of us Hales. Pa unharnesses the team under the long shed, along with all the other horses and wagons from around about.

The meeting house seems half empty these days, with so many men gone away in the militia, for soldiers. But we sing our psalms as loud as ever we can, just as brave as if we was a full company.

Reverend Huntington announces the hymn from the pulpit, and we sing out:

> Come thou almighty King,
> Help us Thy name to sing,
> Help us to praise:
> Father, all-glorious,
> O'er all victorious,
> Come and reign over us,
> Ancient of Days.
> Come Thou incarnate Word,
> Gird on Thy mighty sword,

(73)

Our prayer attend:
Come, and Thy people bless,
And give Thy Word success,
Spirit of holiness,
On us descend. . . .

Surely the Lord God Jehovah can't mistake our call
for help, I'm thinking. For He must know we need
His mighty sword more than *ever*, now.

Reverend Huntington clears his throat and coughs
and sets the dust motes spinning in the shaft of light that
slants in, pale and clear, through the window panes. He
takes for his text the eighth chapter of the Book of
Esther, the sixth verse: "for how can I endure to see
the evil that shall come unto my people? or how can I
endure to see the destruction of my kindred?"

He tells us about the mighty King Ahasuerus who
reigned from India even unto Ethiopia, and of his
Queen Esther, and how Queen Esther was able to
reward the king's faithful councillor, Mordecai, and
how she was able to have the king's evil councillor,
Haman, hanged on a gallows fifty cubits high—the
very same gallows that Haman had built for hanging
Mordecai.

Then Reverend Huntington develops his theme: saying that Queen Esther is like America, who can't bear
to see evil come to her people. And that King Ahasuerus
is like King George III. And Mordecai is like some
Whig fellows, named Burke and Pitt, in London, who
want to help us colonists; and Haman is like Lord
North and the rest of the Tories, who want to do us
harm.

It's cold in the meetinghouse, and the pews crack and

(74)

creak, and I don't follow the whole drift of the discourse. Pa and Brother Enoch say "Amen!" real sharp, when Reverend Huntington prays that King Ahasuerus (that is, King George) will hang Haman pretty quick, and start paying some mind to Queen Esther (that is, to us Yankees).

But with the king's fleet here, and all our militia tearing like mastiffs at the throats of all his redcoats up to Boston, and them growling back, it don't seem likely that Ahasuerus will be listening to Esther *this* spring.

Meeting is so eternal dignified and long! At noontime, we ride back home, where we have us our cold, midday meal. Not *stone* cold, of course, for there's baked beans and brown bread from Saturday's baking left in the Dutch oven—and that's still got some traces of warmth left in it, from Saturday's hot fire. But Pa won't have new fires laid on the Sabbath, nor will he allow fuel to be thrown into the hearth, nor any housework, or cooking, or sewing to be done, nor any lightmindedness, nor any form of chores to be seen to, none whatsoever, from sundown Saturday to sundown Sunday. It's the Lord's day, says he, and he keeps it holy for Him.

We drive back to meeting in the afternoon, and are provided with further solemn instruction from Reverend Huntington, until nearly sundown. Mostly Bible reading, it is, and today he reads us more from Esther. I remember back—a month ago or more—when 'twas Second Samuel, about King David and his son, Absalom.

When the shadows begin to slant across the snow and the reading draws to a close, all the men gather round

(75)

the meetinghouse door to bid each other farewell. The women collect their cold foot-warmers, and herd their children into the wagons. There the patient horses are waiting and stamping under their blankets, blowing out their steamy breath, in the church shed.

Then we drive on home—for a *hot* supper this time —cooked over a roaring, crackling fire.

Mother Abigail wakes me up early next morning, for it's Monday. And this is the day I'm to visit Grandmother Strong and have my very first lesson at weaving at the loom! Nathan must have his length of Holland linen for the shirts he needs, this summer, and he'll want linsey-woolsey for his britches, later on this fall. If I'm to have my part in helping my "bleeding country" preserve her liberties, I must learn to weave strong cloth for the soldiers. And my time to learn is come.

Mother has my breakfast of hasty pudding and milk ready for me today. And after I've et it, she gives me a wicker crate with four live hens in it.

"A little gift for Grandma'am," says Mother Abigail. "The two fat fowl will do her for soup and such. And the speckled pullets will do for laying. I told her yesterday, after meeting, that you'd be carrying them to her, Joanna."

Off I stump in my wooden pattens, through the mud and the melting snow, the crate swinging and the hens cackling.

It's less than a mile to Grandma'am's. There's smoke rising from her chimney. I can see it soon's I come past the big hemlock on the hill. The snow's still clinging thick around the stone walls and under the trees. But on the fields—in patches—the earth is beginning to show through, as if spring was trying to shake off the big white featherbed of winter.

"There's my little girl!" says Grandma'am, when I walk into her snug kitchen. "And see the hens she's brought!"

"A present from Mother," says I.

"Don't clump about in your pattens, dear," says Grandma'am. "Your Uncle Elnathan, and them, are still in their beds asleep, and you'll waken them."

So I take off my pattens, and Grandmother Strong gives me a cup of hot cider against the cold, though it's not all that cold this sunny morning.

"How many lambs has come, dear?" says Grandma'am.

"Well, 'twas three Friday night, and four more Saturday. And I don't know whether 'twas two or three *last* night, for Pa was still asleep when I left the house this morning."

"Oh, Joanna, we must pray the good Lord Jehovah that the flocks be plentiful *this* year, now the army needs the woolens! In the twenty-seventh chapter of the Proverbs of King Solomon it is written: 'Be thou diligent to know the state of thy flocks, and look well to thy herds. For riches are not forever: and doth the crown endure to every generation? The hay appeareth and the tender grass sheweth itself, and herbs of the mountains are gathered. The lambs are for thy clothing.' So sayeth the good book."

"Yes, Grandma'am," says I. "But this year the lambs are not for *my* clothing, but for my brothers who are gone for soldiers against the king."

(77)

"I can't believe you grudge them the wool, Joanna."

"No, Grandma'am. But, while I've been spinning my spools of linen thread, I've tied a book to my distaff, you see. And I've been reading about the troubles, and the siege in Boston, and I've been wondering how it is that Jehovah should allow—"

"Dear girl," says Grandma'am, "you must *never* question the ways of the Lord God Jehovah! We must strive to serve Him, all of us, but we may not question Him, without arousing His wrath. You must *never* be as Job, who questioned the ways of the Lord, only to have the Lord reply to him out of the whirlwind. . . . Do you *know* how the Lord replied, Joanna?"

"No, Grandma'am," says I.

"Then mayhap it should be your *Bible* you tie to your distaff rod, next time you spin! For you should know that Jehovah answered Job's questions not with answers. Nay, but with far mightier *questions*, wherewith Job was overwhelmed, in his own littleness. Struck dumb with the terrible mightiness of God! 'Gird up now thy loins like a man: for I will demand of thee, and answer thou me,' says the Lord, to Job, 'Where wast thou when I laid the foundations of the earth? declare, if thou hast understanding.' And Job cannot answer, and the dread questions of Jehovah pour over him, in a torrent of wrath: 'Hast thou entered into the springs of the sea? or hast thou walked in the search of the depth?' And still Job cannot answer him, and at last he must say to the Lord, 'I know that Thou can'st do everything. I uttered that I understood not; things too wonderful for me, which I knew not,' and Job was *ashamed* for having presumed to question the ways of the Lord God Jehovah. And he repented."

"Then *I* repent, for having questioned them, Grandma'am," says I.

"That's my good girl," says Grandmother Strong.

We go into the loom room, in the ell out back, behind the kitchen. There the huge four-posted machine stands up, solid and tall, like a giant's bedstead.

"Let's see the spools of thread you've spun," says Grandma'am, and I show her the supply I've brought.

"Seems strong and tight, with plenty of spring in it," says Grandma'am. "We'll begin our lesson at the very beginning. First, the loom must be straight and true in all its dimensions, or you'll finish with a crooked piece of cloth, for all your pains. So every thread, Joanna, must be laid on straight and true."

"And where do we begin?" says I.

"With the threads for the warp," says Grandma'am. "The threads that run the length of the goods."

"The warp," says I, repeating after her.

"Now, Brother Nathan needs a dozen shirts," says Grandma'am, "for each of which we'll need two yards of linen. So we should make a bolt of cloth . . . how long, Joanna? Can you make the calculation?"

I remember how to do my sums from the dame school I used to go to—though, now that I can read, Pa's stopped sending me there.

"Twice twelve is twenty-four, Grandma'am," says I.

"Ayeh," says Grandmother Strong. "Twenty-four yards, and one more for good measure. So we'll need

(79)

warp threads twenty-five yards long, or how many feet, Joanna?"

"Three feet to the yard, Grandma'am. I'm no baby! Each thread of the warp, then, is three times twenty-five—or seventy-five feet long."

"That's my good girl," says Grandma'am. "But here's the hard part. How many threads to the warp *entire*? How many threads across, if we weave the bolt one yard wide?"

"Oh, Grandma'am, I don't know," says I, feeling overwhelmed, like Job, when Jehovah catechised him. "How many threads must I lay down to the inch?"

"It varies with the kind of cloth," says Grandma'am. "A fine dimity may have forty or fifty threads to the inch. But our homemade Holland will have no more than a good twenty-five threads to the inch—which is how many threads to the foot?"

"Well," says I, "that would be two-fifty . . . no, three hundreds threads to the foot."

"Perfect!" says Grandma'am. "And that makes nine hundred threads to the yard. So now we must lay on the warp of nine hundred threads. One at a time! Each thread seventy-five feet long."

"Oh, Grandma'am!" says I. " 'Twill be a day's *work* to do so! And I had hoped to begin *weaving* today!"

"There was never any weaving, without *warp*, dear. So let us begin, and perhaps the work will move quicker than you think. You'll be saved the work of measuring off the thread, for I've done that already."

But it's a *nation* of work to lay one single warp thread on a loom, let alone nine hundred! And I'm clumsy about it, besides. First, you must understand the two

(80)

round roller beams. The one at the back is called the warp beam. The one at the front, where you sit, weaving, is called the cloth beam. You must take the twenty-five threads, for your first inch of cloth, and fix them just so to the warp beam at the back. Then you must bring each thread forward, one at a time, through the machinery of the loom. Carefully, so they don't knot or tangle. Then they must be fastened tight to the cloth beam up front.

Oh, it is a *sight* of bother and care! For there are the heddles to worry with. The heddles are two frames, threaded with wires, hanging vertically—one in front of the other—midway in the loom. Each heddle wire— one for each thread—has a loop in the center, through which, Grandma'am says, one thread must pass. It is very ingenious, for the threads *alternate*. I mean, the first thread must go through the loop in the first heddle wire. But the second thread skips the first heddle altogether, and runs through a loop in the *second* heddle. And so we alternate, from one heddle to the other, all the way across the warp.

"The heddles," says Grandma'am, "move against each other. See the two treadles on the floor? Push down on this one, on the right, and the first heddle moves *down*, so, while the second heddle rises *up*. Now, Joanna, attend closely. Do you see what happens? All the *even* threads in the entire warp—in the first heddle —are all pushed down, at once; while at the same instant, all the *odd* threads, the alternating threads, passing through the second heddle, rise up with it, as it rises."

"Oh, Grandma'am," says I, "that's a *beautiful* machine!"

"Stuff!" says Grandma'am. "That's only the heddles! There's a *nation* more for you to learn yet. This be a Yankee-good loom, Joanna, that's wove your mother's shifts and skirts, and your Uncle John Strong and your Uncle Elnathan's britches, many a long gone year! But we got to lay on all this warp, or you never *will* get to throw a shuttle this day!"

Grandmother Strong next shows me how the thread passes from the heddles to the reed—another vertical frame that hangs just in front of the cloth beam. After passing through its proper slot in the reed, the thread is fastened onto the cloth beam, the roller up at the front of the loom.

"We have to make sure that every single thread in the warp is laid on straight. Just so, and in place. So they *all* end up in the same order on the cloth beam, up front, to what they started out, from the warp beam in the back. As the weaving goes on, the finished cloth is rolled up on the cloth beam, here up front, and more warp threads are unrolled from the beam at back."

The beams creak and move as Grandmother Strong stretches the warp upon them.

"Listen to the gudgeons groan!" she says, as the axles of the roller beams squeal.

After we've laid on sixty warp threads, or more, I begin to get the way of it, and the work goes more quickly.

"Laying on a warp is a *world* of trouble," says Grandma'am, "but you must learn how it's done, proper, or you'll never make an *inch* of good cloth. It takes care, same as any other housekeeping task."

As the warp threads increase, the loom begins to look like a giant's harp, and I fancy I can hear it humming.

"Grandma'am didn't mean to speak sharp to you, a while back, about Job and all," says Grandma'am. "But you don't want to get the notion, neither, that you're seeing the *first* troubles the world has ever seen. There's troubles in the world thick as hatchel's teeth, Joanna. And *has* been, ever since Jehovah laid the foundations of the earth, 'When the morning stars sang together, and all the sons of God shouted for joy.' "

"Yes, Grandma'am," says I, threading the seventy-fifth warp thread through the odd heddle, then through the reed, and laying it down, smart and tight and true, right alongside the seventy-fourth thread, and tying it down to the cloth beam.

"The first one of my family to come here to this land," says Grandma'am, "was your great-great-great grandfather, the Puritan Elder, John Strong. He came over here from England, dear, in 1635, to escape the persecutions of the wicked Archbishop Laud, who was then the high and mighty primate of the Church of England. And *he* had troubles aplenty, did Elder John, I can tell you, until he was able to find himself a place of peace and quiet, up to Windsor, on Connecticut River. He lived to be ninety-four, *my* grandma'am, Freedom Strong, used to say."

Grandma'am makes sure I haven't twisted the thread, and goes on with her story.

"His sons," says she, "had to fight the Pequot Indians, in a terrible bloody rising. That was in my grandfather Jedediah's day. And then, in my own father's day, Preserved Strong *his* name was, there come the fearful French and Indian Wars. Why, the very year I was born, Joanna, my family was living up in Northampton, Massachusetts, then, on Connecticut River. And in that very year, 1704—seventy-two years ago—the French and Indians swooped down on Deerfield, in the deepest deep of winter, when snow was drifted up over the palisades, and chopped their way into the houses. Scalping folks, and burning down half the town, and carrying a world of half-froze captives over the snowy mountains to Canada. Some were killed outright, with tomahawks. Some never *did* get back home to Zion again. And some, like Eunice Williams, lived out their lives married to Indian braves. Eunice *loved* her husband, too. *Wouldn't* leave him, even when her brothers begged her to. That's what my mother told me. Tabitha Lee, she was, before she married Father."

"Then," says Grandma'am, "in *my* time, come the last great war for Canada, and the fighting at Louisburg fortress, up on Nova Scotia. And now, there's fighting once again—this time round Boston. *Every* generation has its troubles, dear. We can't escape them or ask why they come. We can only put our trust in the Lord God Jehovah. For as the Psalm says: 'In the time of trouble he shall hide me in his pavilion: in the secret of his tabernacle shall he hide me; he shall set me up upon a rock.' "

"Oh, Grandma'am," says I, "I hope and pray that he may."

Our troubles today *do* seem to be overwhelming troubles. But then I see Grandma'am's firm, tired mouth, and I think about the Indians chopping through

(84)

the doors of the houses in Deerfield when she was a baby. And I begin to understand that there never *will* be a time when we won't need to be brave.

By the time we have seven hundred strands of the warp in place, it's midday, and Grandma'am says we must stop for our meal. I don't see much of Uncle Elnathan and them, for they're out back in the barn, now, mending harness. It's just Grandma'am and me, with our corn chowder and our toast and apple butter and our hot cider.

"You say you been reading, Joanna?" says Grandma'am.

"Yes," says I, "at my spinning wheel. Brother Enoch has a book to home he borrowed from Reverend Huntington, called *Common Sense*—same as he read from, two weeks ago at meeting."

"Ayeh," says Grandma'am.

"And 'fore he left for Winter Hill, Brother Nathan told me I must keep after my reading real *diligent*, so's I could advance my learning, same as any boy. . . ."

"That's just what Nathan *would* advise," says Grandma'am, with a wise nod, and a little smile.

"So, I kept at it, and I read it all. It says we had best *part* from Britain, and set ourselves up for free and independent, even if a great fleet of warships comes over here to chastise us. For he says we have it in our power to begin the world *over* again, Grandma'am! Just like the Lord God Jehovah did, in the Beginning!"

"So that's Common Sense, is it?" says Grandma'am. "And maybe it's *good* sense, too. Even though we have to go through dangers for our liberty, clustered thick as hatchel's teeth. Nothing worth having comes *easy*.

(85)

Neither good linen. Nor good butter. Nor good cheese."

Then Grandma'am asks me when Dr. Sam has to go back to the army, where he's a surgeon. I tell her I don't know for sure when Dr. Sam's leave is up, but that Sister Rose and Little Joe will move back into Pa's house, and close up her own house, just as soon as Dr. Sam has to depart.

Grandma'am tells me to be sure to kiss Little Joe for her, and I promise I will. Then I say it's time we get back to our weaving, because I don't want this day to close without my having thrown a shuttle—after waiting all these years. Grandma'am smiles at me and says, "That's my good, diligent girl."

We set to work with a will, and I've got so skillful now that in no more than an hour or so, I have all the remaining warp threads tied and stretched in place. All *nine hundred* of them! A full yard wide, twenty-five threads to the inch, knotted and true, every one of them threaded through the proper heddle, just as they should be.

Now I have the fanciful notion that the loom looks like a sturdy grape arbor, with a vine spreading its tendrils, ready to grasp, and put out leaves, and bear fruit.

Press down on the right treadle, and the front heddle dips, and four hundred and fifty threads sink down, and the alternating four hundred and fifty rise up, leaving a perfect v-shaped valley between the two banks of stretched threads.

Press down on the left treadle, and the second heddle dips, and all the threads that were down rise up, and all that were *up* sink down, behaving in perfect harmony and unison. Like waves, strung out on the harp of the sea. Rise and fall. Rise and fall. Beautiful and regular as ocean waves.

Grandma'am sees I'm pleased, but she shakes her head and says, real mild, "This is the very *simplest* kind of weaving, Joanna, using but two heddles. There's *pattern* weaving, you know, with three and four and five and six heddles, and a world of different colored threads. And instructions all wrote out on paper, that look like music for part-singing of the psalms! Master weavers know how to *follow* them instructions, and they can weave stars and daisies and crosses and crowns and the good Lord knows *what* all kinds of beautiful patterns and shapes. Weave them right *into* the cloth, just like they was telling a story! So don't you be all puffed up with pride over this simple country loom. With our unbleached brown linen, and the simplest, plainest kind of common weave."

"Oh, Grandma'am!" I say.

"And still," she smiles, "no reason to be crestfallen, neither. We'll make us a fine, good, sturdy cloth for Nathan."

Then Grandma'am shows me how the weft threads is laid in—the cross threads—from off the wooden shuttle. It's a hollow, boat-shaped piece of polished elm wood, with a spool of linen thread inside it, that feeds out of a hole in the shuttle's side, unreeling, as the little boat rides back and forth across the waves of the warp. For you throw the shuttle from one side of the loom to the other, passing it through the v-shaped tunnel the heddles make, in the linen warp threads.

(87)

Once the shuttle is across, and the thread taut, you pull the reed up, sharp, against the weft thread you've just laid in. And the beater, or rod, fastened to the bottom of the reeds goes "thump," and pounds the weft thread tight in place against the finished cloth, before you.

Then you press down on the left treadle, and *that* heddle goes down, and the other comes up. Another v-shaped tunnel is formed in the warp threads. And you throw the shuttle back through that. And you beat the new weft thread into place, with a "thump" of the beater.

And so the rhythm begins: right treadle, throw shuttle, *thump;* left treadle, throw shuttle, *thump;* right treadle, throw shuttle, *thump;* left treadle, throw shuttle, *thump.*

And there, before your eyes, the strong tissue of brown cloth begins to grow. Like a living thing. And your fingers begin to fly. And the loom creaks and groans and thumps. Like a galloping horse. Or a ship, rising and groaning and tossing in the sea.

Right treadle, throw shuttle, *thump.* Left treadle, throw shuttle, *thump.*

The boat-shaped shuttle skims back and forth across it's v-shaped wave. The moving strands of the linen sea rise and fall, and seem to take on a surging movement all their own. I beat the weft into place, and throw the shuttle, and raise and lower the heddles in a sleepy, happy way. It's *worlds* better than churning, or spinning, or sewing, or milking.

This is the work a *grown woman* should do, I'm thinking. I begin to think I'm telling some kind of

(88)

story *myself*, written right into the web I'm weaving. Weaving! Making cloth. Here's a shining stretch of useful, bright linen, where before it was only a tangle of yarn!

Right treadle, throw shuttle, *thump!* Left treadle, throw shuttle, *thump!*

There's something mysterious, something exciting, about the creak and hum and rattle of the loom.

Grandma'am is asking me about the new house Pa is planning, and whether we've heard from Nathan. And she tells me of the hives of bees she's aiming to start, and the new cheese-press Uncle Elnathan is building for her. I answer as polite and regular as I can. But the strange new music of the loom is in my head, and my eyes are on the band of linen that grows wider and wider, at my own creation.

Right treadle, throw shuttle, *thump!* Left treadle, throw shuttle, *thump!*

Inch after inch unreels from the shuttle as the little boat rocks its way back and forth across the linen waves. The shadows begin slanting farther and farther across the floor, for the February afternoon is short. And soon the sun is hanging like a red-hot coal, caught in the gridiron branches of the naked elms. Hanging there, a prisoner, at the edge of our snowy field.

"Well, now, Joanna," says Grandma'am. "That's a good two yards of linen for today. You'll have your cloth for Nathan's shirts in no time."

"Is it *sound*, Grandma'am?" says I.

Grandma'am plucks at it, and frowns. "It's sound," says she. "A mite pulled, here and there. And a bit rough on the selvage. But a *fine* turnout of linen!"

And I jump up from the loom, and I kiss and hug her, hard. And we say good-bye, and I start home. I'm thinking I've become a weaver, and a woman. And the clack and the rhythm of the loom is singing in my head as I run through the shadows in the snowy fields. It isn't until I'm under the naked pear tree in Pa's dooryard that I remember I've left my wooden pattens on Grandma'am's hearth. And *that's* the reason my felt slippers have got sopping wet, all through!

PART THREE

But One Life to Lose

ALL THROUGH MARCH AND APRIL I keep busy weaving good brown Holland linen. But there's been so many things happening to Nathan, *important* things, during this time.

Here, in Coventry, we've seen the pussy willows put out their silvery buds, and the jack-in-the-pulpits come springing up in the marshes. Windy March, with her pale green shoots, and her fat red buds on every shrub and tree. And rhubarb poking up close to the margin of the meadow brook. And all those fleecy new March lambs.

We hear the news from Boston—how Nathan's guns from Fort Ticonderoga have been dragged across country and set up on Dorchester Heights, overlooking the city. In consequence, British General Howe thinks he'd do well to pull out, before all those guns start blasting. So he's heading for Halifax, Nova Scotia.

March seventeenth is the day he leaves, and we call it Evacuation Day. The redcoats quit Boston at last, abandoning hundreds of ruined buildings, and a half-wrecked city. We hear there are hundreds and hundreds of folks there still sick with the smallpox.

Nathan writes to Brother Enoch, saying that his regiment broke camp on the eighteenth, and that they were heading down through the Connecticut River valley, for Lyme, and then on to the waters of the Sound. We're told that five regiments of soldiers have gone by water from New London, down to New York.

I overhear Father and Brother Enoch talking it over. Since Howe left Boston, General Washington must figure that the British soldiers plan to strike *another* American city, pretty soon. And that city seems likely to be New York. So General Washington is moving most of his soldiers from up around Boston down to Manhattan—either marching them twelve days across country, or sending them down to New London, where ships can transport them down Long Island Sound. Seems as though Brother Nathan was one of the lucky ones to be sent by water.

There's so much to attend to here on the farm that nobody scarcely has time to notice my birthday, on the nineteenth of March. That's the day I become twelve years old, and Mother Abigail says, "Look at our big grown-up girl!" Father kisses me, and Grandmother Strong sends me over a little tub of maple sugar, for a present.

These days Mr. Nathan'l Wright's two teams of oxen —his wicked reds and his well-behaved duns—are churning up our fields and roads. They're hauling granite in heavy stone boats, or sledges, from Mr. Wright's quarry to our cellar hole. Work has begun in earnest on the new house. Mr. Wright and his masons are cutting stone and building us a cellar and two heavy stone piers. And they'll be followed by some fireplaces and two chimneys stout enough to last for many a lifetime.

I watch the masons building the two stone piers—the supports in the cellar that will buttress the two big chimneys. They're so strong and mighty they make me think of Job and Jehovah, when they was arguing about who was laying the foundations to the earth. I never *see* such power in stone! Those huge, upthrusting curves, and all that strength! Father must be building to outlast the ages. As if he too—and not just Thomas Paine—was ready to begin the world over!

This new house of ours is going to be as stout and as solid as granite and oak can make it. Oak and granite and all of us Hales, together, working just as hard as we can.

It's mighty amusing to see Mr. Nathan'l Wright coaxing and coddling his teams of oxen, dragging their heavy sledges of stone. He knows Father won't let him whip the beasts, and he has promised to abide by Father's rules. But I can see it costs him a *power* to keep his promise! And if I wasn't Father's obedient daughter, I think I'd agree with Mr. Wright that Reprobate and Papist and Fire and Brimstone and Sin and Satan would be more than a *mite* improved by a lick or two of the willow switch.

Brother Enoch receives a little note from Brother Nathan—"Brother Captain" is what Enoch calls him now—toward the end of April. Nathan writes he's in barracks, now, in New York City. What a huge metropolis it must seem to him, I'm thinking. A place of twenty *thousand* souls! What are these little Connecticut villages of ours, with their few hundreds, compared to a great city of that size! Only Philadelphia and Boston

(97)

and Charleston can be any larger. And Nathan never inside any one of them!

I take Little Joe with me, and sit outside under the big pear tree, just beside the house. The pear tree Father planted, soon after he and Ma was married. It's covered with snowy April blossoms, now. The bees keep murmuring through them, as if they knew a secret best kept by themselves alone.

There's robins and all manner of birds building nests in every tree. And oxen bellowing, hauling stone for Father's cellar. And grapevines putting out shoots and tendrils. And the men ploughing in the fields, where flax and buckwheat and Indian corn will be sowed later on.

" 'Sweet lovers love the spring,' " says Grandmother Strong, to nobody in particular. For she's walked over to call me back to my weaving. For the twenty-five yards of linen are still not woven yet, entire. And we promised the shirts for Nathan by summer, and Grandma'am won't let me forget them.

How lovely it would be this spring—with the cellar building, and the pear tree blooming—if it weren't for this war! Six of my brothers gone for soldiers, and who knows how long they'll be gone!

Brother Enoch, the man of God, says we must put our entire trust in the justice and mercy of the Lord God Jehovah. Many a morning he takes his adze and his pegs and his mallet, and spends the day whacking away at the framing timbers of the new house. Some days there's a neighbor to help him.

It's being pieced together section by section—like a giant geometry problem—spread out on the grass around the cellar hole. And Hales and Strongs and Adamses and neighbor friends come from around about to lend a hand.

But Nathan can't be here to help us. Nor Dr. Sam, nor Brother John, nor Brother Samuel, nor Brother Joe, nor Brother Richard, nor Brother Billy. I can't help but sigh thinking how fast this house might have risen up, if all of them could have been here, helping. As they would have done, gladly, if it weren't for King George and his redcoats.

Brother Enoch always reads us the letters he receives from "Brother Captain" Nathan, in New York City. But his letters aren't too frequent, and they take *ten days* to get here. Mother Abigail and Grandmother Strong and Sister Rose and Sally and Alicia and all of us gathered at the supper table love to hear the news they contain.

Early in May came a letter from Nathan telling us how General Heath reviewed his brigade—Knowlton's brigade—on the green, near the Liberty Pole. That happened back on April 2nd. Then he writes of General Israel Putnam's arrival in New York, on the 4th of April, annoyed to find some British warships—the *Asia* and the *Duchess of Gordon*—moored right out in the Hudson River, with the city under their guns! With Tories in the city supplying the ships with fresh meat and eggs and vegetables! And Tory governor William Tryon safe on board the *Duchess of Gordon,* along with his rich Tory friends, the DeLanceys and the Apthorpes, and the Bayards. All of them Tories who had to run away from their elegant homes, once our American troops marched into New York.

Nathan's letter told us that General Washington didn't get to the city until the 13th of April, and Mrs. Martha Washington arrived there, from Virginia, four days later. The city is still full of Tories, Nathan says. And the colony of New York ain't *yet* in favor of separating from King George, no matter what *Common Sense* may advise.

He informs us that a big inn there—that used to be called the King's Arms—is now known as the Province Arms. Of course, that's because King George has fallen so low in popular favor with most of us, by now, except among his Tory friends. Nathan says the inn has a big cupola on the roof, from where you can see Staten Island and Brooklyn, and all New York harbor.

He's been to Bowling Green, where he's seen a gilded statue of King George, riding on his horse, dressed up like a Roman emperor. An emperor with a laurel crown, such as Cato or Plutarch might have known! A Roman emperor, wearing a toga, and wielding his royal sceptre over us all.

May passes sweet and peaceful on the farm, like April. All the orchard trees pink with blossoms. Violets thick as can be, along the brook in the sheep meadow. Sister Rose tells Mother Abigail and Grandma'am that she's going to have another baby, and I overhear the three of them whispering about it. She and Dr. Sam will have a new brother or sister for Little Joe, says she, sometime this November. I'm real glad for Sister Rose, and she seems happy, too.

I finish weaving all the linen we'll need for Brother Nathan's shirts, and Grandma'am shows me how to wash and stretch and bleach the cloth. It feels strong and substantial in my hands. I take much pleasure in remembering all the hours I spent at the labor, throwing the shuttle, working the heddles, slamming the beater, seated at Grandma'am's loom.

Father takes a similar pleasure, I feel sure, watching his new house grow. Mr. Nathan'l Wright's men are nearly through stoning the cellar. Almost all the heavy oak framing timbers have been squared and adzed and pegged and fitted.

All our relatives and friends and neighbors have been invited to the big house-raising on the 4th of June, and Brother Enoch has rid out as far as Captain Robinson's inviting raisers to the gathering. Meanwhile, Grandma'am and Sister Rose and Mother Abigail and Sally and Alicia and me, we been sewing shirts for Nathan. Each of us making two, so he'll have a full dozen from the linen I wove.

We hear from Asher Wright that Nathan and some of the rest of the soldiers in his brigade have been playing football, on the Common, down to New York. Asher said in his letter to Mr. Wright that Nathan can kick that ball high, high up. Right up over the tops of the trees!

End of May and beginning of June there's a *world* of preparations in store for all us womenfolk, here on the farm. Getting ready for all those hungry workers, coming to the house-raising. We have pies and bread to bake, and doughnuts to fry, and stews and puddings

(101)

to fix, and crocks of baked beans to prepare. There's to be more than sixty hands here, on the 4th of June.

The day of the big event comes and goes in a whirl of activity. Such hammering and grunting and sweating and calling out! Oxen stamping and bellowing. Men laughing and joking and singing. Everybody busy as can be, but enjoying themselves, too.

Once the frame has been raised up and pegged tight, 'bout midday, we women set out the food on long tables under the trees. And we run back and forth to the kitchen in the old house, bringing out pitchers of milk and water and cider, and loaves of bread, and platters of hot food.

In the afternoon, the men begin raising the roof. About six o'clock in the evening—when the ridgepole is raised and fitted and finally pegged in place—there's a nation of hollering and cheering and singing. Father serves out rum and hard cider and cherry brandy to all the men that want any. And there's feasting and joking and congratulations and carousing till way after dark.

All this happens on Tuesday, June 4. Two days later, June 6, is Brother Nathan's birthday. He's twenty-one years old, and Father remembers him special, that night, when he says grace before supper.

The Sunday after, at meeting, the Reverend Huntington thanks the Lord God Jehovah for having permitted the frame of the house of His servant—Deacon Richard Hale—to go up so rapid and so solid, with injury to none. Then he prays real earnest that the Lord God Jehovah will further grant us a similar indulgence in the setting up and raising of our new *nation*.

But, in truth, none of us expects that *that* will be

accomplished without terrible toil and loss and sorrow for us all.

"Brother Captain" Nathan writes from New York that he's heard news that the delegates to the Congress down in Philadelphia are arguing and striving to get a unanimous majority declaring for independence. But they are a *long* way from coming to any such agreement, so far. Much less to any *unanimous* agreement.

Brother Nathan writes Enoch that a mob collected in the city on the night of June 10, angry because there was still so many Tories still left free to roam about as they pleased. The crowd caught six or seven, and tarred and feathered two of them. Couple more was rode about on rails, and beaten and abused. All of them mistreated and paraded up and down until General Mifflin and General Putnam made the mob turn them Tories loose.

Nathan told us, too, that he's been to a hanging. It was a Yankee soldier, named Thomas Hickey, who was one of General Washington's guard. He was having some traffic with the Tories, they say. There was even rumors that he'd plotted to *murder* General Washington! Nathan couldn't tell us much in his letter. But all the Yankee troops was paraded out to see Hickey hanged on June 28, at eleven in the morning.

Brother Enoch saw to it that Brother Nathan's twelve linen shirts was bundled up real careful, and dispatched to him at his barracks. They was sent to him by way of a soldier friend of Enoch's who was passing through Coventry, on his way to New Haven, and then by water to Washington's army in New York. Alicia Ripley put

(103)

in a letter for Nathan, along with the shirts. And so did me and Grandma'am.

There's big news from down there these days, and most of it bad. General Howe's fleet of ships from Nova Scotia sailed into the Narrows on the 29th of June. A *forest* of British warships he had with him! More than a *hundred!* The biggest armada this continent has ever seen! As if all London were afloat, and tramping ashore, over here, to oppress us poor colonial rebels! Only the Lord God Jehovah knows how many redcoat soldiers there are aboard those ships. All of them armed, and setting up camp now, on Staten Island. Nathan says they hear there's even *more* ships and redcoats on the way, from Britain.

We expect to hear of a terrible big battle down there, in New York City, all too soon. I'm praying regular every night, now, for Nathan's safety.

Yesterday, at supper, Father told us all that he'd heard that General Washington had written to our Connecticut governor, Jonathan Trumbull, asking him to send him just as many soldiers from our state militia as he could possibly spare. Governor Trumbull said the most he could scrape up was maybe five hundred men. That's three regiments. And he wasn't sure that he'd have muskets enough for them all.

General Washington is very fond of Governor Trumbull. He has a nickname for him. It's "Brother Jonathan."

We're real proud of him, too, here in Connecticut. He's the only governor in *all* the thirteen colonies who's sided with us Americans. The British hate him, and call him "the Rebel Governor." But we rebels love

(104)

"Brother Jonathan," because he keeps on wearing himself out, raising men and supplies and food and arms for General Washington's army. He's got a son who's a soldier, too. A paymaster, down in New York. Nathan knows him.

There's a rumor says General Washington is so uneasy now that the British fleet has come, that he's going to send Mrs. Washington back south, to Virginia.

Early in July, another letter comes to Enoch from "Brother Captain" Nathan, telling how all the soldiers is sweating in the heat, digging entrenchments in Brooklyn, and on both banks of the East River, and on Governor's Island. And all along a line of defenses on Grand Street. They can't understand why General Howe hasn't attacked them yet. But Howe and all his men, him and that forest of British ships, are poised, ready for battle, waiting there at Staten Island.

Here on the farm in Coventry, the men are putting floors into the new house, and riving shingles for the roof, and sawing clapboards. Brother Enoch has been much fretted, riding to and fro to Norwich and Glastonbury, trying to buy nails for the new house. Now, with this war on, there's shortages of copper and lead and iron and I don't know what all. And nails are in mighty short supply.

The new flax is springing up from the linseed Grandma'am sowed about a month ago. The fields are heavenly blue with waving flax flowers. There's swarms of bees buzzing in them, and even thicker in the buckwheat flowers. Except for the sound of hammering and sawing and the lowing of cattle now and then, and the bleating of sheep, everything's peaceful and quiet. Fra-

(105)

grant, too, with hot July sun on the new-mown hay. And the piney scent of fresh split shingles hanging heavy in the air.

One such hot afternoon, early in July, we hear what happened down in Philadelphia, on the Fourth. How the bells was rung, and the Declaration was read, separating us *officially* from the tyrannous King George III.

Nathan writes Brother Enoch that on the night of July 9th, at sundown, General Washington had the Declaration of Independence read out, at the parade ground, so that all the troops could hear it. And a few hours later, a mob of New Yorkers pulled down that big statue of gilded lead—King George's statue—and hacked it all to pieces. They're planning to melt it down for bullets for us Yankees! I wished I'd been there to see *that* spectacle!

I've been watching a nest of robins in our pear tree. Now, in mid-month, all the fledglings have learned to fly, and soon the nest will be empty.

We hear from Brother Nathan that our bundle of shirts arrived safely, and he tenders his thanks to all and sundry for remembering him, and he sends his special compliments to Grandmother Strong. Nathan really dotes on Grandma'am. And she on him, for that matter.

Alicia don't really come out and *say* so, in so many words, but I believe she must have heard from Nathan, too.

Brother Enoch will be riding down to New Haven, to be there on the twenty-fifth, so's he can attend the Yale College commencement exercises. While he's at commencement, he's going to make sure he talks with Mr. Dwight, the president. Brother Nathan is anxious to have a copy of his Yale degree, and has wrote to Brother Enoch asking him to secure it for him.

Toward the end of the month, when the flax will be ripe, Grandma'am and I will walk down the rows, uprooting the plants, one by one, and laying them down to dry. It's a *nation* of work, preparing flax!

The linseed pods, up at the top of the stalks, must be combed out, one by one, with a kind of wooden comb, called a rippler. We save part of the seeds for planting, next year, and we press oil from the rest, and feed the husks to the cattle.

The flax stalks have to be tied in bundles, called "heads," and stood upright in a pond, buried four or five feet deep, underwater, and weighted down with sods and stone. That's so the stalks can soak real good for a couple of weeks, so the fibers will separate easy from the wooden core, that Grandma'am calls "the shove."

As if that ain't enough to keep us busy, we got to get the sheep sheared, and begin washing and combing fleeces. Nathan's going to need some linsey-woolsey britches this fall. We *promised* him a pair. And a world more of Washington's soldiers will need woolens, too. And Pa means to have every scrap of wool from this farm—like he's said over and over—saved for the Yankee army.

There's lots *more* to fixing flax than I have thus far related. After it's been rotted—or "retted," as Grandma'am says—for a couple of weeks, underwater, the

(107)

bundles must be taken up out of the pond, opened up, and spread out to dry.

Then you must begin separating the fibers from the core, first by smashing the stalks on a flax brake. Next they must be scutched, or beaten, with paddles called "scutchers," till all the fibers separate from the core. Then all the fibers must be drawn through a prickly cluster of slender metal teeth—called heckles, or hatchels—till all the impurities and kinks are combed out, and the little broken pieces of tow have been separated from the "line," or the "lint" as Grandma'am calls the good, long fibers that remain. Then, and only then, can you begin spinning your thread on the wheel!

So much trouble preparing flax for spinning that sometimes we invite neighbor women in—to scutching bees, and heckling bees—to make the tasks go quicker.

Brother Nathan writes Brother Enoch that he hears that twelve French ships of the line are in St. Lawrence River, near Quebec.

And Brother Enoch, back from Yale College commencement, sends Nathan a copy of the college degree he earned three years ago. Like he promised he would.

Early in August, Brother Enoch rides up to Hartford hoping to find nails for the new house. He wanted to buy some white lead, for paint, too. But he doesn't have any success.

Mother Abigail is just delighted with this new house Father is building. The men have nearly finished putting on the clapboard sidings. And they'd have finished

(108)

shingling the roof, too, if Brother Enoch had been able to find more nails for them.

We've got our window sashes and wooden shutters, but no window glass, as yet. King George put a tax on window glass—same as he put on tea—and Father wouldn't *touch* that glass any more than he would drink the king's tea. Now that we are a separate nation of our own, I 'spect Father will be willing to purchase some *Yankee* window glass. But try and find any!

Brother Enoch receives a letter from Brother Nathan, late in August, telling us that there was a terrible thunderstorm in New York City on the night of the 21st. They think that a big battle is coming soon.

Rumors come up Long Island Sound a few days later, saying that General William Howe ordered his redcoats to land on the Brooklyn shore on the 27th, and that General Washington's troops crossed over, from Manhattan, to meet him. Our side was *terribly* defeated, we hear, with more than 1,200 prisoners taken, and over 400 killed and wounded.

"Lord have mercy!" says Grandmother Strong, real earnest and severe, when Father prays for Nathan and all my other brothers, these nights at the supper table.

Alicia Ripley is sad and silent and white-faced. And Sister Rose and Mother Abigail and I, we been crying over our spinning. Sick with worry.

We hear there was a heavy fog the night of the 28th of August, right after the Battle of Long Island. And in that fog, General Washington and his troops slipped back back across the East River, onto Manhattan Island again. But we *know* they won't be able to hold New York City, after that terrible defeat. They'll have to retreat soon as General Howe and his redcoats decide to invade from Brooklyn.

And where will General Washington and Brother Nathan go then?

It's hard to realize that Brother Nathan may be in battle, now. Wounded. Or even killed, maybe. Here's all this corn standing ripe in our peaceful fields. Apples half-red in the shady orchard. The fruit so thick and heavy that the trees must bow down their heads, their branches sweeping the grass. Just the way a maiden hangs her head over, when she's washing her tresses.

August slips away, and so does the rest of summer. September harvesting keeps all the men busy. Us womenfolk have pickling and preserving to do, and apple sauce to make. Hogs to butcher and hams to cure.

When we're not peeling fruit or curing meat, we're busy spinning woolen yarn, and knitting, and weaving. Any day now we expect to hear that General Washington's army has had to leave New York.

It used to take Nathan's letters ten or eleven days to get up here to the farm in Coventry from New York. But ever since that big battle back in August, travel is all disrupted, and the mail is more uncertain than ever.

We hear rumors that the British have entered New York and burned the city. Others say it isn't so. But *nothing* is sure.

Father has a letter, over two weeks old, from Nathan. It is dated September 13. Nathan tells us that his commanding officer—Lieutenant Colonel Thomas Knowlton of the Connecticut Rangers—said that General Washington had asked for volunteers. Wanted an officer to volunteer to go behind the enemy lines on Long Island, and find out where the British troops were disposed. Nathan told Father in his letter that he was going to go! "I leave tonight, perhaps to return, perhaps not," says he. My handsome brother, Nathan, in so much danger!

Father prays a long, long time to the Lord God Jehovah the night we get this letter. All of us women—Alicia and everybody—have wet handkerchiefs and red eyes when he gets through.

"Lord have mercy on us all," says Grandma'am. And even Little Joe says, "Mercy!"

Little Joe will be two years old this month, on September 17th. And Sister Rose's new baby will come, she expects, by mid-November. Grandma'am believes she's right, by all the signs.

Despite the terrible worrisome news, we women must keep busy with our woolens and our harvesting. The men are plastering ceilings in the new house. When all the walls and floors are finished, they'll start dismantling *this* house we're living in, now. For this old home of ours will be pulled down, and all the wall-panelling, and doors, and widow-sashes from here will be used in the new place. That's the way we Yankees are. Thrifty. "Use it up. Wear it out. Make it do," we say. And it's as good a maxim as any, I suppose.

On Wednesday, October 2nd, Brother Enoch rides up to the dooryard. He dismounts near the pear tree, by the kitchen door, looking terrible worried and downcast. He's heard the worst kind of alarming rumors about Brother Nathan. Heard them up to Granby, where he was visiting our relative, Reverend Strong.

Enoch tells Father and all of us, at supper, that he talked to a soldier, up from New York. A sergeant who said he'd heard that Captain Hale, belonging to the east side of Connecticut River, near Coventry—"Captain Hale in Knowlton's outfit, the one they call Congress' Own"—said that Nathan had been seen to *hang*! Within the enemy lines, he was, in New York. Having been taken as a spy, reconnoitering the British lines.

Such moans and outcries as went up from our unhappy family!

Father spoke real sharp to the Lord God Jehovah, saying he hoped this awful news was without any substance whatsoever.

But we're all so *troubled* by what Enoch heard that none of us can sleep. And Brother Enoch will be riding off, as soon as he can secure a proper pass for travelling, to go down to Westchester County. To see what better news of Nathan he can come by!

We learn that the rumors were *true* about General Howe. He *did* land in New York, at Kip's Bay, on September 15th. And he drove all the Yankee troops northwards, up past Harlem, up to the forts on the northern heights of the island, overlooking the Hudson.

Nathan's commanding officer, Lieutenant Colonel Knowlton, was killed in battle the very next day after the landing. And how many more of us will have to suffer and die, I wonder, before "the birthday of a new world," is *truly* at hand?

How can this October sky be so bright and blue? And all those pumpkins lying in the fields, so fat and placid? With my brother Nathan hanged for a spy! Brave and handsome as Nathan is . . . just turned twenty-one.

Alicia and Grandmother Strong and Sister Rose and Sally and Mother Abigail and me, we all try to be cheerful and hopeful. With all the confusion this war brings, nothing's certain sure, until the news is confirmed. We keep trying to believe that Brother Nathan may still be safe, and we pray with Father, every night at supper, asking the Lord God Jehovah, in His infinite mercy, to spare Captain Nathan Hale.

There's more terrible news from New York. It's now sure that an engulfing fire swept the city, near a month ago, in September. About a week after General Howe invaded. Nearly a third of the buildings was destroyed, we were told.

Then Brother Enoch receives this dreadful letter from his minister friend, Dr. Waldo. Letter says that last month on the 15th of September—about a week before that terrible fire in New York—Captain Nathan Hale disguised himself as a Dutch schoolmaster, wearing brown knickerbockers and a linen shirt and a broad-brimmed felt hat. He was answering General Washington's call for a volunteer to go spy out the British positions on Long Island.

Father read Dr. Waldo's letter out loud, for all of

us, the same night Brother Enoch brought it home—
Wednesday, October 16th.

"Why did he have to volunteer for a spy, Richard?"
says Grandma'am. "Wasn't he in danger enough, as a
soldier?"

"Letter don't say, Mother," says Father. "But you
know Nathan well as I do. He must have had sufficient
reason for wishing to do so. Nobody could have forced
him to volunteer."

"Nathan! Nathan!" says Alicia Ripley. And I can't
bear to look into her face.

"Letter goes on to say," says Father, trying to steady
his voice, "that his friends, Asher Wright and Sergeant
Stephen Hempstead, left camp with him, at 8:00
o'clock at night, from Harlem Heights, Sunday, September 15th. Nathan knew he was in danger, so he gave
his watch and most of his papers, and his silver shoe
buckles to Sergeant Hempstead. The night was foggy.
And the three of them went up the Sound, to Norwalk,
Connecticut. Next evening, Monday, September 16th,
Nathan said good-bye to his two friends, and one of our
little sloops took him across the Sound to Huntington,
Long Island."

"Lord have mercy! My poor brave boy!" says Grandmother Strong. All I'm thinking is that Nathan must
have been wearing one of *my* linen shirts, when he put
on that schoolmaster disguise.

"All of us must understand," says Brother Enoch,
"that Dr. Waldo is reporting *rumors* in this letter. Ever
since the Battle of Long Island, British troops been
confiscating livestock and property from every rebel
farm on Long Island. And rebel refugees have been

streaming across the Sound, to Fairfield, and Bridge-port, and Westport, and all the Connecticut coastal towns. Ever since General Washington's defeat. But everything's *confusion*, and nobody knows for sure what's happening on Long Island."

"There's still a chance for Nathan?" says Sister Rose.

"There's a *chance*, Lizzie," says Father, real heavy and slow. "But it seems to me a small one. I fear the boy is lost. Dr. Waldo writes Enoch that Nathan had finished his work—but before he was able to get off Long Island and deliver his papers, he was betrayed, took up by the redcoats, and hanged without cere-mony!"

Such a wail goes up from everybody as I can't de-scribe.

All of us at the table begin clamoring and weeping. Only Father remains stern.

"Listen to me!" says Father. And a dead hush falls. "Dr. Waldo says that one of our *own* Long Island cousins, Samuel Hale, may have turned Nathan in! We *know* he's a Tory, but Dr. Waldo don't know for sure whether this story's true. I don't believe it, myself. But then, I don't know *what* to believe. All I know is we may have lost Nathan. And Enoch can't even start off for General Washington's camp, down in Westchester, until next week. So we probably won't know what's *really* happened until way on into November."

I know I mustn't ask Grandma'am *why* this could happen to us. Or *why* it could happen to Brother Nathan. For she'd look stern and set her chin and talk to me about the Book of Job.

I know just what she'd tell me: if you question the ways of the Lord God Jehovah, He turns your questions inside out, and wants to know: "Wast thou there when I laid the foundations of the earth?"

But what kind of answer is that? And what does it have to do with Brother Nathan?

Only thing we can do, while we're waiting to hear, is keep on helping with the work here on the farm. And keep on fixing up the new house.

The men are pulling this old one down, now, right over our ears. All the windows and doors and floors and panelling have gone from the old, into the new, and we'll be moving in very soon. How happy this day could have made Mother Abigail and all the rest of us Hales! If it weren't for what we fear for Nathan!

Father receives a letter from his brother, Major Sam Hale, who lives up in Portsmouth, New Hampshire. Uncle Sam wants fresh news of Nathan, but Pa puts the letter by, for the time being, because he don't know what to answer until Brother Enoch gets home safe.

We hear there was a big battle down to White Plains on October 28th, and General Washington lost again. We think Brother Joseph may have been in it, and Brother Nathan, too, if he's still alive. Even Brother Enoch, the man of God, may have been swept up into the fray, if he had reached the vicinity of White Plains, time the fighting began.

By the time Brother Enoch gets back home, winter has set in, full. It's November 6, and the air is chill.

Every tree—even the oaks—has given up its leaves. The sky is bleak and somber—a dull steel gray. Gray, sad, and forbidding.

Everything we was afraid of seems to be true. My brother Nathan has been dead, since September! All the while we been hoping, he's been dead and gone!

Father's face don't quiver while Enoch tells us the awful news. We're all of us seated around the hearth in our grand new house. There's apples roasting in front of the fire, and black walnuts and chestnuts. There's a high, whiney winter wind blowing through the bare branches of the shagbark hickory out front.

The story is simple and dismal enough. Nathan was captured on Long Island Sound, near Lloyd's Neck, by twenty British marines. They was from the British guardship, *Halifax*, Captain Quarne commanding. This was the night of September 20th, so Enoch tells us.

Enoch had all this from some officers in Nathan's old regiment. Knowlton's regiment it used to be, but since he was killed, commanded now by Colonel Webb.

Captain Quarne took Nathan prisoner, and sailed him down to General Howe's headquarters, on East River, in Manhattan. Howe was staying at Mount Pleasant, the big country house that belongs to James Beekman.

They say the redcoats found papers and plans and drawings and estimates of British troop strength hidden beneath the inner linings of Nathan's shoes!

Brother Enoch talked to two of Washington's young officers, Captain Alexander Hamilton, and Captain William Hull. Hamilton told him that it didn't take

General Howe very long to realize that Nathan was a spy. So General Howe talked with my brother a short while, in the Beekman parlor. And he sentenced him to hang, the next morning, in front of the British artillery park, where all their cannon was assembled.

Brother Enoch says that Nathan was kept under guard that night in Mr. Beekman's greenhouse. Nathan wanted to talk to a minister, but they wouldn't let him see one. Then he asked for a Bible, but they wouldn't let him have that comfort, neither.

Only man who was kind to him was a British officer, Colonel John Montresor. He gave him paper and pen, to write some letters home.

Enoch thinks that Brother Nathan *may* have written letters to us, on that dreadful evening. But we have yet to see them.

The very night of Nathan's capture nearly *half* of New York City went up in flames. It seems that it was Yankees set the fires. We don't know for sure. They say the fire was awful, with nearly five hundred houses burned.

All we know for certain is that next morning, Sunday, September 22, Nathan was led out under a tree, and stood on a cart, while the redcoats put a noose around his neck. That handsome neck, standing out of his collar like a tall, proud column!

They asked him what he wanted to say, before he died. And he replied—just like he read to me, out of Addison's *Cato*:

"I only regret that I have but one life to lose for my country."

Then they pulled the cart out from under him. And let him struggle and die.

Just because Nathan's dead don't mean the war is over for the rest of us. While Brother Enoch was off to Washington's camp in Westchester, he saw Brother Joseph and Brother Billy. They told him that during the Battle of White Plains, back in October, a bullet passed through Brother Joseph's clothes so close it might have killed him.

We're going to have to suffer ever so much more sorrow and trouble before we win our liberty, and can start our new world over—no matter how easy Mr. Paine makes it sound in his *Common Sense*.

We hear that Asher Wright will be paying us a visit, bringing home Nathan's deerhide trunk, with all his shirts and things.

I keep thinking how Alicia is never going to be Mrs. Captain Nathan Hale. And how Little Joe ain't never going to play "Hoss-ee!" no more with Nathan jumping into a line of cider barrels. Nor will I be reading *Cato* with him, in the early morning.

There's nothing much you can say or do. Not when you loved somebody as much as we loved Nathan. Father says he's going to plant twenty-one sugar maple trees—one for every year of Nathan's life. He's going to set them out right in front of our new house, just across the road.

Father wants Reverend Huntington to write an epitaph for Nathan, for a memorial stone tablet that we want to set up in the churchyard.

Pa never cried for Nathan, that I saw. But we know he took it hard. Mother Abigail says she saw the letter he wrote to his brother, Sam, up in Portsmouth—all about Nathan. Here's what Pa wrote: "He was a child I set much by. But he is gone."

And he was wearing one of my linen shirts when they hanged him.

Alicia and Grandmother Strong and Sally and Mother Abigail and I sat up all night last night, while Sister Rose was having her new baby. Dr. Sam ain't here. He's still off with the army.

Today's Monday, November 18, 1776. Lizzie's baby is a nice, fine boy! All of us womenfolk have gathered around her, in the best bedroom in Father's new house. It's November, but it isn't gray today. The sky is a bright, bright blue.

Grandma'am brings in some strong beef tea for "dear Lizzie." The baby's finished nursing, and he's sleeping peaceful beside my sister.

And I say, "Sister Rose, how you going to name him?"

"Why, Joanna," says she. "What do you suppose? I'm going to call him *Nathan*. Nathan Hale Rose."

ABOUT THIS STORY

In writing this work of fiction about Nathan Hale, I have relied heavily on five books: *Under the Guns: New York 1775–1776* by Bruce Bliven, Jr., Harper & Row, 1972; *Nathan Hale, the Martyr Spy* by Charles W. Brown, J. S. Ogilvie Co., New York, 1899; *Nathan Hale: 1776* by Henry Phelps Johnston, Yale, 1914; *Documentary Life of Nathan Hale* by George Dudley Seymour, New Haven (privately printed, 628 pp.) 1941; and *The Life of Captain Nathan Hale* by Isaac William Stuart, F. A. Brown Co., Hartford, 1856.

Almost *everything* important we wish to know (or to believe) about Nathan Hale seems to be a matter of intense controversy among his biographers.

Consequently it seems easiest to begin with the facts which are *not* in dispute. His father, Deacon Richard Hale (1717–1802) of Coventry, Connecticut, first married Elizabeth Strong (1727–1767) in May 1746. To them, twelve children were born: Samuel, John, Joseph, Elizabeth, Enoch, Nathan, Richard, Billy, David, Jonathan, Joanna, and Susanna. Susanna and Jonathan died as infants, but the other ten grew to maturity; six of the eight boys who survived fought in the American Revolution. Two years after his first wife died, on June 13, 1769, Deacon Richard married his second wife, Mrs. Abigail Adams, widow of Capt.

Samuel Adams of Canterbury, Connecticut. They had no children. But one of Abigail's daughters by her first marriage—Sarah Adams—married Nathan's older brother John, in 1771. Her second daughter, Alice, was living with the Hales, too, at this time. Enoch and Nathan were both very fond of "Alicia," as they called her; but, at her mother's urging, on February 8, 1773 (while Enoch and Nathan were still going to Yale) Alice married a well-to-do elderly neighbor, Mr. Elijah Ripley. They had one child—Elijah—but by the time this story begins (in December 1775) both the father and son were dead, and Alicia was a young widow. Whether Alicia ever became secretly engaged to Nathan Hale is a matter of considerable dispute. But, more of that later.

Joanna Hale (1764–1838) who tells this story, was twelve years old in 1776. There seems to be no reason to doubt that she adored her handsome, athletic, twenty-one-year-old brother, Nathan. At the age of twenty, in 1784, she married Doctor Nathan Howard, of Hampton, Connecticut, and she died at age 74. It is a matter of record that Nathan wrote home from New York, thanking his *elder* sister, Elizabeth ("Sister Rose") for his linen shirts, but *fiction* has allowed little Joanna to weave the linen from which they were made. I would like to believe she did so, but cannot prove it.

Nathan Hale, himself, (June 6, 1755—September 22, 1776) seems to have struck all his acquaintances, relatives, and friends as being a remarkably personable, attractive, forceful, and lovable young man. His mother, Elizabeth (who died when he was twelve) wanted him to become a minister. (His brothers Enoch and David *did*). In 1769, he and Enoch went off to Yale, together; and in 1773, at the age of eighteen, Nathan received his degree, with honors. After serving as a schoolmaster in a little one-room school, in Haddam, Connecticut for a bit more than a year (during which term he championed the rights of women to an advanced education), Nathan enlisted, and found himself a lieutenant in Washington's army, besieging Boston, in the fall of 1775. He visited his family in Coventry in December and January. In February, he was back in camp outside of Boston. In March the British evacuated the city; and in April, Hale was sent to New York, with the rest of the American troops, and remained there until his death in September. Almost everything that happened to him from September 13–22, 1776, during the last week of his life, is cloudy with hearsay, and scarred with controversy.

For example: On June 28, 1976, the *New Yorker* magazine carried an article by Eugene Kinkead ("Our Local Correspondents: Still Here") which referred to Nathan Hale. It quoted from a plaque originally affixed to a building at First Avenue and Forty-sixth Street (but now at the Yale Club, at Vanderbilt Avenue and Forty-fourth Street) which reads, in part, "At the British Artillery Park near this Site, Nathan Hale, Captain in the U.S. Army, Yale Graduate of 1773, Apprehended Within Enemy Lines While Seeking Information, Was Executed on the Morning of September 22, 1776. His Last Words Were 'I Only Regret That I Have But One Life To Lose For My Country.'" The article goes on to say: "Historians differ as to whether the British artillery park was near the location on First Avenue, or farther north by the Dove Tavern, near what is now Third Avenue at Sixty-sixth Street. They also differ as to whether the famous statement was ever actually uttered by Hale."

Indeed, they *do* differ about these and many other matters concerning Nathan Hale! Stuart and Johnston (cited in the first paragraph of this note) feel sure that Hale was secretly engaged to his step-sister, Alice (or "Alicia") Adams Ripley, the widow of Elijah Ripley. And they assert that he gave her a miniature of himself, in a silver locket. Mr. George Dudley Seymour (also cited above) is equally certain that there was *no* engagement, and *no* locket. As a romantic, I chose to follow Messrs. Stuart and Johnston, in this matter. But none of us will ever *know*. (Some years after Nathan's death, Alice was courted by Brother Enoch, the man of God, but she would not have him. Later she married a Mr. William Lawrence, and lived to a ripe old age).

Perhaps—as Seymour suggests—there never *was* a locket containing a miniature of Nathan Hale. Members of Alicia's family later said that there *was* one, but if it existed it is now lost. And even the silhouette (which may still be seen on the old pine door) may not actually portray Nathan Hale—though a number of members of the Hale family, in the nineteenth century, felt sure that it did. If the shadow portrait *isn't* genuine, then no pictorial record exists, and no proof remains of his handsome features—except for the verbal testimony of many contemporary ladies of the Connecticut Valley, and New Haven, who spoke of him admiringly indeed.

Quite a different matter, however, from the question of Alicia Adams Ripley, is the *rest* of Seymour's *Docu-*

mentary Life. It is an invaluable book, reprinting Enoch Hale's *Diary,* Nathan Hale's army diary, his letters, and much, much more. Without it, I could never have written this story.

To return to further controversial matters: I doubt that we shall *ever* know, for certain, the particulars of Nathan Hale's capture and execution. The British Colonel John Montresor discussed these matters, verbally, with Washington's young officers, Alexander Hamilton and William Hull, and the latter wrote about them, many years later. But Nathan Hale was, after all, on a secret mission, and the British apparently left no detailed documents as to his actions and utterances, at the end. All we have is Col. Montresor's fairly reliable hearsay, transmitted many years later, through Hull.

It is more likely than not that Nathan Hale *had* read Addison's very popular play, *Cato*—but it is not certain. He may have been betrayed by a Tory relative on Long Island, but his own father wasn't absolutely sure that the story should be believed. It seems impossible that we shall ever know the certain truth of the matter, today.

We aren't even going to know, for a certainty, whether or not he ever said: "I only regret that I have but one life to lose for my country." But we can be sure (from what we *do* know) that he lived and died in perfect consonance with that lofty sentiment, whether he happened to speak those words or not.

This book has not been written, however, to encourage young people to *die* for their country. It is much more important that they should live worthily for it, and for themselves.

(125)

The most touching document I read, in the course of my research on this book, was Deacon Richard Hale's letter to his brother Samuel Hale, in Portsmouth, New Hampshire, in which he discusses Nathan's death. It is full of a father's lasting regret for his dead son, and it is worth reprinting here in full:

Dear Brother

I Rec'd your favor of the 17th of February Last and rejoce to hear that you and your Famley ware well your obversation as to the Dificulty of the times is very just so gloomey a day wee niver saw before but I trust our Cause is Just and for our Consolation in the times of greatest destress we have this to sopert us that their is a God that Jugeth in the earth if we Can but take the Comfort of it as to our being far advanced in life if it do but serve to wean us from this presint troublesom world and stur us up to prepare for a world of peace and Rest it is well the Calls in Providence are loud to prepare to meet our God and O that he would prepare us

You desired me to inform you about my son Nathan you have doubtless seen the Newbery Port paper that gives the acount of the Conduct of our kinsman Sam'l Hale toard him in York as to our kinsman being here in his way to York it is a mistake but as to his Conduct tord my son at York Mr. Cleveland of Cape Ann first reported it near us I sopose when on his way from the Armey where he had been Chapling home as what was Probley true betra'd he doubtless wass by somebody he was executed about the 22nd of Sepetember Last by the Aconts we have had. A Child I sot much by but he is gone I think the second trial I ever met with

my 3rd son Joseph is in the Armey over in the Jarsyes and wass well the last we heard from him my other son

(126)

that was in the service belonged to the Melishey and is now at home   my son Enoch is gone to take the small pox by enoculation   Brother Robinson and famley are well   we are all threw the Divine goodness well   My wife joins in Love to you and Mrs. Hale and your Children

Your Loving Brother
Richard Hale

Coventry March 28th 1777

In later years, Deacon Hale set up a memorial stone to Nathan, in the graveyard in Coventry. The inscription is thought to have been written by Rev. Joseph Huntington; it says, in part, that "Nathan Hale, Esq., a Capt. in the army of the United States . . . resigned his life, a sacrifice to his country's liberty, at New York, Sept. 22, 1776."

Deacon Hale never planted the grove of sugar maples mentioned in this story, but twenty-one trees were later set out, by a Hale descendant, early in the nineteenth century.

One final certainty: Enoch Hale's diary attests that Deacon Richard's new home was indeed raised on June 4th, 1776. It may still be visited today in Coventry, Connecticut.

F.N.M.